THE HOLLOW TREE CHILDREN

BOOK 1

PATRICK WALLIAMS

Copyright © Patrick Walliams, 2017

Published by Acorn Independent Press Ltd, 2017.

The right of Patrick Walliams to be identified as the Author
of the Work has been asserted by him in accordance with the
Copyright, Designs and Patents Act 1988.

All rights reserved.

This book is sold subject to the condition it shall not, by way of
trade or otherwise, be circulated in any form or by any means,
electronic or otherwise without the publisher's prior consent.

ISBN 978-1-912145-14-0

Acorn Independent Press

Tom, Minna and Finch are, it has to be said,
not your average children, and the forest
they live in is not your average forest.
Beany (a not-very-good magician), is their
grandfather. He keeps an eye on the three of
them from time to time and tries,
not always with success, to keep
things under control.

CONTENTS

BOOK 1

BOOK 2

TOM, MINNA AND FINCH

Tom, Minna and Finch were three of the weirdest kids you are ever likely to see. *How, you may ask?* Well, their hair was very long and tangled, they wore clothes that were ripped, patched and faded, and they hardly ever wore shoes. That was because they spent lots of their time climbing about in the trees. *What else made them different?* Well, they lived alone in the forest and they never, ever, went to school – never!

They lived in... yes, lived in... an oak tree, *which had* grown from an acorn planted by a red squirrel nearly a thousand years ago. It was one of the oldest trees in England, and it was completely hollow.

The downstairs room, which belonged to all of them, was *JUST* big enough for the kids, but was a bit of a squeeze when Beany came to stay. There was not really enough room for stairs, instead several ladders led to the upstairs rooms. Tom, Minna and Finch had

made all the furniture themselves from wood they had found in the forest

Tom who was the eldest, and Finch, the youngest, shared the bedroom halfway up. Minna had a room to herself right at the top... only it wasn't really the top, living above her were a pair of barn owls, and above the owls there lived a family of bats. The bats were very noisy, especially at dusk when they went out to hunt for moths in the forest.

The treehouse had beautifully carved doors and windows, which Beany... their grandfather... had made. He had his own little house, his 'hide-away', somewhere on the other side of the forest. He was a magician... of sorts... I say that because he wasn't a very good magician, at least he wasn't a very good magician all the time, and sometimes his spells, as he sadly admitted, "went a bit wonky".

Last year, for instance, there had been a cricket match in the village and the Cricket Club had asked him to stop it raining. They had even paid him some money, but no sooner had he cast his 'stop the rain' spell, then down it came, even heavier. There had been a dreadful flood and, worst of all, a thunderbolt had hit the Clubhouse roof and set it on fire! Luckily no one was hurt.

When the family ran out of money completely, which they did quite often, Beany would go off and join a travelling fair or circus and perform his magic tricks there. His 'headless man' act was quite famous. He would rub his secret Moonshine onto his face and into his hair and then, when his head had vanished completely; he would dance about and sing funny songs... WITHOUT A HEAD! Old ladies screaming in terror would faint, but children just loved it.

One fine summer's day, while Beany was away on his travels earning some money, Tom, Minna and Finch climbed up into their Lookout Tree, a beech tree, which was the tallest tree in the forest. There they were, at the very top, more than one hundred feet above the ground. If they looked one way, they could just see the village; if they looked the other way they could see the high hills on one side and the dark heart of the forest on the other. Nobody ever went to the dark heart of the forest, for it was dark and gloomy, even at midday, and dingbats lived there, and even ghosts, so they say.

"Where do you think Beany is today?" Finch asked dreamily. He was sitting on a branch a hundred feet above the ground and swinging his legs happily.

"Furze Fair probably," said Tom, "doing his magic tricks."

"I wonder if he'll bring us presents like last time?" Finch went on.

"Of course he will, he always does!" said Minna. For Beany would always bring them back, "a few little luxuries", as he called them: trainers, T-shirts, coconuts… things like that.

Finch was now hanging upside-down from the branch.

"That's funny!" he said suddenly, looking over the treetops.

"What is?" asked the others.

"I think I can see him!" said Finch. He was staring at a distant clearing in the forest. There was a tiny, weenie figure, right in the middle. Tom and Minna stared. "However can you tell it's him?" they asked at last.

"Because I've got super-human eyes," Finch replied confidently, "and being upside-down makes them even better!"

All three began to scramble quickly down the tree. They dashed along, in the dappled sunshine between the forest trees, splashing through the little rivers and streams, not stopping until they got to the clearing. Long grass, almost as tall as they were grew in the clearing and butterflies and bees whizzed and buzzed about them.

"Come on, let's give him a scare!" said Tom, and they began to sneak their way silently through the grass. When they were really close they all rushed forward together with a great shout... and then they realized their mistake and fell about laughing. It was a scarecrow!

"Well, it does *LOOK* like Beany," said Finch, and the others agreed.

"And the hat is a lot better than the one that Beany wears," said Minna, "I'm taking it back for him." She carefully took the hat off the scarecrow, tipped the spiders out without hurting them, and rolled it up neatly.

Then they flopped down in the grass and sprawled there in the lovely sunshine. Soon they were all asleep.

And it was while they were happily dozing that Beany leaped out on them with a mighty yell. "I thought I'd give you all a scare!" said he. Now it was Beany's turn to fall about laughing. When he had quite finished, he produced a big brown paper parcel that he had hidden in the grass. "A few little luxuries!" he said.

"And we've got something for you too!" said Minna shyly, presenting him with the rolled-up hat.

"Crikes! What a beauty!" Beany said, putting it on immediately.

The others crowded round, admiring it.

"Better than my old thing any day!" Beany added. "Pity to throw it away though. How say you we give it to the old bird-scarer, he looks a bit down on his luck?"

After that, they all tramped back in the direction of the tree house and, while they tramped along, as happy as bees, Beany told them about his latest adventure. He told them how he had spent that night in his 'hideaway' and how he had been woken early in the morning by the police!

"There were loads of them," he said, "and some on horseback too, and they were led by their boss, Chief Constable Dunstable. And there were dogs too. And all because I didn't have a licence to practice my magic. Well, my secret passage had fallen in, you see, and there was no way out!"

"Whatever did you do?" asked Minna.

Beany laughed. "I gulped down a whole bottle of Moonshine!" he said. "A whole bottle in one go! And I vanished completely! The dogs could see me, of course, and wagged their tails, and the horses could see me too, but they just looked at me with their kindly eyes and didn't let on. But the best bit is the last bit because, just as they was leaving, I jumped up behind Chief Constable Dunstable, on his lovely black horse, and we galloped all the way back to the village, me sitting right behind him all the way, holding on for dear life. All the way back he was yelling: 'Keep your eyes peeled for that Beany What's-his-face, lads, I just KNOW he's near, I can feel it in my bones!'"

Beany laughed so much at his own cleverness that he had to stop and wipe his eyes on the silk handkerchief that he always kept in the top pocket of his tattered old jacket. In no time they were back at the tree house.

ROCK-DIAMONDS

For days on end, Tom could think of nothing but Moonshine. He wanted some for himself and he pestered Beany again and again to give him some. At last Beany became quite cross. "When I was your age I had never even heard of Moonshine," said Beany, "and I certainly never had any of my own to muck about with!"

But Tom persisted. "At least tell me how it's made," he said.

"Well, it's not that difficult to make," Beany admitted, "because all you need is a mirror and a Rock-Diamond and, when the Moon is full, you reflect the moonlight onto the Rock-Diamond. When the drops of Moonshine begin to form on the crystal, you must catch them in a little bottle. Remember to put a stopper on the bottle though, because otherwise it will all fizzle away before morning."

"And where do I get a Rock-Diamond from?" demanded Tom.

Beany sighed. "Well, that's the difficult bit," he replied. "Only the Hill-Demons have got Rock-Diamonds. And you know very well what Hill-Demons are like. If you go anywhere near them they'll come after you. They'll rip your head clean off more than likely. Just remember what happened to your cousin Billy... poor little soul."

Tom wandered off and thought his thoughts and planned his plans. He knew exactly where the Hill-Demons were. They lived in the high hills and once, when Tom and Finch were there, looking for fossils, they had sat down beside a mountain stream to cool their feet in the rushing water. And they had seen a little cave there.

At first they had thought nothing of it but, after a bit, they had heard the strangest sounds coming from it: wild, crazy music. Shouting, cackling laughter. Tom and Finch had abandoned their shoes and fled for dear life. They had never gone back.

For nights on end Tom dreamed about Moonshine and Hill-Demons and Rock-Diamonds. And about Moon-Diamonds and Rock-Demons and Hill-Shine and Moon-

Demons... everything had got mixed up in his dreams. But the more he thought about it, the more determined he became to return to the cave beside the rushing water. He would go when the Hill-Demons were asleep and off-guard. He would get some Rock-Diamonds for himself.

The thought of those precious crystals had made him brave. So one night, when the others were asleep, Tom, who had been tossing and turning for hours, threw off his bedclothes, got dressed, and scrambled quickly down the ladder.

"Are you going out?" Finch asked sleepily.

"Of course not, you idiot, go back to sleep!" hissed Tom.

Tom sped out of the house and darted barefoot between the huge forest trees. They looked even more huge in the starlight, but they were his friends and gave him confidence. He paused in the middle of a clearing and could dimly see the outline of the High Hills against the stars.

He wished, for a moment, that Finch had been with him for company. But Finch would slow him down. And anyway, it wouldn't be

fair. Finch was younger and smaller and could not run so fast. What if the Hill-Demons should catch him?

Tom dashed off again, jogging along silently beside the stream. It was wide and slow moving at the bottom of the hill but, as he went up, it got narrower and faster... and there were lots of little waterfalls along the way. When he got to the cave he sat down and rested for a while. He wished that Finch and Minna were there too. But they would only have held on to him, and Minna (although she was not the eldest) would have said: "You are not to go in Tom! I absolutely forbid it!"

Tom took a deep breath and went in. The cave was narrow, and the passage was twisty and steep. In fact it was so steep that, once or twice, Tom lost his footing and slid and slithered downwards on the loose stones. He could hear far-away music playing... wild, uncanny music. THRILLING music!

It was dark down below, but not QUITE pitch dark because Rock-Diamonds give off their own pale light, which is a bit like moonlight, and Tom could see that ahead of him there were four or five passages leading off to the left and right. One of them had rusty old iron railway lines along it with rusty old iron trucks with the letters XZKQ painted on their sides. But the music came from another, smaller, passage and that was the one that Tom chose.

The music fascinated Tom, and drew him onwards. Soon he came to a rusty iron door. There were two guards slumped by it. At first Tom thought they must be dead, because they lay there so very still... and there were insects running about all over them. But they were just drunk, just very, very, very drunk. Tom stared at them. They were the first Hill-Demons he had ever seen.

They were quite small, a bit like monkeys (only they didn't have hair of course) and their faces were a bit like goblins, (with pointy noses and chins), and a bit like people, too. They were wearing baseball caps, back-to-front, with the letters XZKQ on them. Tom sneaked round them very carefully and crept into the cavern beyond.

It was lit with little gleaming lanterns, and the music was loud and crazy. There were sacks, like big old-fashioned coal sacks, standing in rows all along the sides. And the sacks were stuffed full of opals and jades and tiger's eyes and Rock-Diamonds. The Rock-Diamonds were easy to spot because they gave off their own flickering light. Tom stuffed handfuls of them into his pockets. He should have left there and then... but he didn't. He wanted badly to see who was playing that thrilling, amazing, fantastical music. So he sneaked along, hidden from the demons by all those sacks.

There was some sort of party going on up the far end of the cavern. There were demons everywhere... hundreds of them. They were gulping down inky black wine out of pewter mugs and gobbling up red stringy meat out of pots. The lady-demons had long black hair braided with rat's tails and snakeskins, but the men just wore wrong-way-round baseball caps with the letters XZKQ emblazoned on them.

As he got closer the music became deafening, and there was a lot of shouting and swearing and singing and dancing going on. And quite a lot of fighting, too, with plenty of punching and scratching and kicking and biting. But then the fighting would stop, and

25

the dancing would start again. Tom could see an ancient demon with a face like a monkey sitting on a luminous rock and playing a violin. Tom adored the music and stared, fascinated, at the violin. And the more he stared at it the more puzzled he became. For he could hear trumpets and drums and flutes and whistles and marimbas and, well, anything you can think of! But it all came from that one fiddle.

Suddenly the music became tired and lifeless, and the old fiddle player took a bottle from the rock beside him, shook it carefully, and poured some liquid into the instrument. And then he sloshed it round and round and started to play again. And all those trumpets and drums and whistles and accordions could be heard again. Tom had a violin at home, and he wanted that bottle... badly. He was determined to have it!

He moved forward cautiously... but not cautiously enough! A sack of Opals tipped over and fell with a crash. The music stopped. A thousand eyes were upon Tom. For a moment, nothing happened. But then they all rushed at him.

"Get him! Grab him! Seize him!" they yelled. "Rip his head off!"

They would have caught him, but all those opals had rolled everywhere, and the demons slipped and skidded and tumbled and fell all over the place. Tom had never been so terrified in his life. He ran full tilt along the passage and leaped over the guards in one single bound (they were still asleep) and began to scramble up towards the world above. The demons were close behind him though, snatching at his clothes and grabbing at his feet and ankles as he scrambled, like a mad thing, up that tunnel.

Once they DID grab him, but they had been drinking and were not steady on their feet, and the one who had grabbed him fell over, and the one behind him fell over *him*, and the one behind *him* fell over *him*, and the one behind *him* fell over *him*, and the one behind *him* fell over *him*, and the one behind *him* fell over *him*, and the one behind *him* fell over *him* and the one behind *him* fell over *him*, and the one behind *him* fell over *him*, and the one behind *him* fell over *him*, and the one behind *him* fell over *him*, and the one behind *him* fell over *him*, and the one behind *him* fell over *him*, and the one behind *him* fell over *him*, and the one behind *him* fell over *him*, and the one behind *him* fell over *him*, and the one behind *him* fell over *him*...

But they picked themselves up and came after him again. And they WOULD have caught him just after he left the cave if he had not been very lucky. A demon threw himself at Tom and grabbed hold of his ankle and Tom fell JUST where the hill was steepest. He hit the ground running at full speed. And immediately he began to roll.

And he rolled over sticks and stones and anthills and molehills. And every time he rolled over an anthill or a molehill he would bounce up in the air and then he would bounce down again going twice as fast as before. You must remember his pockets were stuffed full of Rock-Diamonds and this gave him extra weight and extra speed.

When the Hill-Demons saw what was happening they too threw themselves down on the grassy slope and went rolling after him. Or TRIED to, but Hill-Demons are really, really skinny and light, and every time they crashed into an anthill or smashed into a molehill they came to a full stop and had to start all over again. But Tom was going faster and faster every second.

Before he knew it, he was at the bottom of the hill lying in the lovely long grass. How peaceful it was!

He got up gingerly (he was still a bit dizzy) and patted himself all over to make quite sure he was still in one piece, and that the Rock-Diamonds were still in his pockets. Then he set off, whistling and singing (and limping a bit, too) all the way home.

"Whatever's happened?" asked the others in amazement when Tom climbed painfully up into the treehouse JUST as the morning sun was rising up above the treetops. For he was covered all over with bumps and bruises and cuts and scrapes and gashes and grazes. The others were really shocked.

"Crikes," exclaimed Beany, "get them plasters Minna!"

When Tom told them where he had been and what he had done they didn't, at first, quite believe him, so he shoved his hands into his pockets and tugged out the stolen Rock-

Diamonds and banged them down on the table. They glowed like embers in a fire.

"Crikes!" said Beany, for the second time that day. "But tell me this, Tom, why in the name of Heaven, did you risk your precious life robbing those wicked creatures when you could have used lumps of sugar like I said... coz they're just as good?"

"You never said sugar lumps were just as good!" he said quietly, and his face turned very red.

"I'm sure I did though!" Beany mumbled and now Beany turned very red. "Well, I certainly MEANT to. Good Heavens. Silly me."

Later, when he was sure no one was looking, Tom hid his precious crystals under the floorboards where he was certain nobody would ever find them.

BABY LEO

It wasn't long after the Rock-Diamond episode that the owls left the oak tree. One night they went out hunting as usual and they never came back. Had they found somewhere else to live? A barn, perhaps? Or a church steeple? Nobody knew for sure.

Minna was sad. She loved to hear them moving about up above her and calling to each other, but Finch was pleased. He was fed up sharing a bedroom with his brother and badly wanted his own room in the space that the owls had lived in. He begged Beany to make one more ladder so that he could move upstairs and, eventually, Beany agreed. He had a razor-sharp axe and could quickly cut down trees and shape them into anything he wished.

So one morning Finch and Beany set off for the forest together, Finch with a saw, Beany with an axe. They soon found two straight, slender ash trees that were just perfect and soon they had cut them down and begun to shape them. But suddenly, Finch let the saw fall to the ground.

"Oh!" he said.

"What is it?" asked Beany, looking up.

"Dingbats!" whispered Finch, his eyes wide with terror.

"Where?" yelled Beany, dropping the axe.

Both of them were suddenly running to the nearest tree and they were quickly half way up. The next moment, roaring and bellowing, a horde of Dingbats, about twenty of them, came charging after them through the trees. They charged straight up to the tree where Finch and Beany were hiding.

Their big red dribbly mouths were wide open, and they stared up into the tree with their short-sighted, watery eyes, as they snuffled and churned up the ground with their queer-looking hooves. One or two of them tried to jump up into the tree, but they fell and rolled over onto their backs.

Next they started biting each other and then they stared at each other. They were very, very smelly. Finch and Beany, high up in the tree, kept perfectly still and did not make a sound.

Suddenly one of the Dingbats made a horrible screaming sound. He was the biggest one, and had greeny-yellow teeth. Up they got again and, the next moment, they were charging away through the forest, roaring and bellowing, with their horrible tails stuck out behind them like broomsticks.

Beany and Finch looked at each other. They didn't say anything for a while. Then Beany winked at Finch, and Finch giggled. They had both been seriously scared.

"They won't be back today," said Beany at last.

Slowly and carefully they climbed down from the tree. They could still smell the horrid smell of the Dingbats, which is a bit like gunpowder fried in garlic. Beany's axe and Finch's saw had been trampled into the mud. But they were both in a merry mood now. Fear, (once you've got over it), makes you feel jolly.

They laughed and joked as they walked back to the treehouse, but looked over their shoulders now and then to make *QUITE* sure they were not being followed. The first thing they saw when they got back was Beany's old beaten-up pram: the one he used for gathering sticks and firewood in the forest. Minna and Tom were leaning over the pram looking into it.

"Shush!" Minna whispered urgently, "don't wake him up!"

Beany and Finch looked into the pram and in the pram was a little baby Dingbat. It had a little piggy nose and was fast asleep.

"Oh lor!" said Beany.

"Wherever did you get it from?" asked Finch.

"I found him in the hedge this morning," replied Minna proudly. "He was crying and squealing, isn't he sweet?"

Finch looked quickly at his sister to see if she was joking.

"He's a bit sweet," he said doubtfully.

"I couldn't just leave him there, crying and squealing, now could I?" said Minna.

Finch shook his head. "No," he said.

"There'll be trouble!" said Beany with a sigh and he went indoors to look for his pipe and herb-tobacco and he shut the door.

The new baby spent most of the time asleep. When he *DID* wake up he cried and squealed, and Tom and Minna and Finch would give him milk from an old baby's bottle they had found in the lane; and then they would take it in turns to push the pram up and down over the bumpy grass among the trees. They decided to call their new baby Leo.

"There's no milk left!" said Minna one day, "we shall have to go to the village. Leo's hungry."

"Oh lor!" said Beany, "do be careful. You know what they're like in the village."

Tom and Minna and Finch made the pram look as smart as they possibly could. They washed all the mud off it, and covered up the holes and cracks with pieces of material and stickers. They even tried to dress the little baby Dingbat up in some old dolly's clothes, but he just wouldn't keep still and cried and squealed even more. In the end they covered him up with a pink and silver baby-blanket, plonked a pink and gold baby's bonnet over his head and off they went to the village.

The wheels squeaked loudly as they trundled the heavy pram along the village street, and people peeped and peered at them through their windows as they passed by. Finch, who had extra keen hearing, was able to make out what they were saying, even though the windows were shut. Things like: "There go those weird kids again – the ones that live in the forest! Look how little they are! And goodness me, just look at their clothes! Poor little mites! Why don't that Beany What's-his-name dress them proper?"

Finch wanted to shout rude things at them, but he said nothing, and contented himself with squinting, rolling his eyes and pulling faces instead. It was Tom and Finch who went into the shop. Their pockets were stuffed with coins, most of which they had found in the lane: "Baby-milk please," they said, spreading the coins out on the counter.

Minna stayed outside minding the pram, jigging it up and down and hoping – just hoping – the baby wouldn't wake. Several people tried to look in and one very old lady with a shopping basket came up *REALLY* close.

"And whose little baby is that, deary?" she asked.

"Mine," replied Minna firmly, staring defiantly at the old lady and holding tightly to the pram.

"Oh surely not," said the old lady with a little giggle. "Is she your little sister then?"

"No! Actually he's my baby," said Minna obstinately, jigging the pram up and down again and staring at the old lady boldly. The old lady stooped low over the pram.

"Oh, do let me see!" she implored, taking hold of the pink bonnet. And then Tom and Finch came out of the shop with the baby-milk.

"Don't you touch his bonnet, 'coz if you do he'll get the sunburn!" yelled Finch rudely.

But it was too late! The old lady lifted the bonnet and she let out a shriek.

"Oh oh oh! The nasty creature! It's one of them 'orrible nasty forest creatures! One of them nasty 'orrible forest creatures that do smell so 'orrible!" she shrieked.

People came running up! They were so NOSY! They all wanted to have a look in the pram! Leo woke up and began to cry and squeal in terror. Tom and Minna and Finch all grabbed hold of the pram and began to run with it as fast as they could. The pram was extra-heavy with all those tins of baby milk in it, and it bumped and bounced about all over the place.

"Stop thief!" Someone shouted, (I don't know why), and several people got knocked over or bumped into each other and just *FELL* over.

Tom and Minna and Finch didn't stop. When they got home that night they were tired out. One of the wheels had come off the pram. But baby Leo, sucking on his baby-bottle, looked happy and pleased.

Leo grew bigger and bigger every day and he was very clever. They taught him to do all sorts of tricks – how to whistle and how to stand on his head, and things like that.

During the day he was very happy but, at nighttime, especially when the moon was full and the Dingbats could be heard roaring and squealing in the forest, he would become distressed.

"Oh lor!" Beany would say. "There'll be trouble, I know there will!"

One night, in late summer, the moon seemed extra big and bright and red, hanging low in the sky like a great big ripe apple. Tom and Minna and Finch were in the treehouse, leaning out of the window and staring at it. Beany was there, too, gazing up at the moon and smoking some of his new herb tobacco. Leo was fast asleep on Minna's bed.

"Why is the moon so special-looking tonight?" asked Finch.

"It's what's called a harvest-moon," replied Beany happily. "You get them at summer's end, when the apples be ripe and the corn is ready for harvesting!"

And then suddenly, far away, they heard a bellowing and a roaring and a squealing.

It was the Dingbats again.

"Hope they're not coming this way!" said Finch nervously.

"Oh, we're safe enough in our oak tree-house," Beany said, puffing his pipe contentedly.

But the roaring and the bellowing got louder.

"Oh, dear, they're coming this way," said Minna.

"Here they come!" exclaimed Tom a moment later.

And, roaring and bellowing, the Dingbats came charging through the forest. There were at least thirty of them and they came charging up to the treehouse, bellowing and squealing and staring up into the branches with their little piggy eyes.

Leo woke up and started running round and round in circles squealing and crying. Minna grabbed him and tried to calm him.

Outside in the moonlight some of the Dingbats started leaping up, high in the air, and biting off great big chunks of bark from the tree, and then down they would tumble. And then up again they would leap, snapping and snarling.

And then Beany tried to do one of his magic spells to calm them. He spread out his fingers towards the Dingbats and spoke some magical words in a loud, spooky sort of voice... but this only made them worse. It drove them into a frenzy and they *ALL* started leaping up, high in the air, roaring and bellowing.

Minna had been holding Leo very tightly, but suddenly he gave a most enormous

WRIGGLE and he leaped right out of her arms and headfirst he went out of the window and away into the moonlit night. Minna let out a wail, but all the Dingbats were suddenly quiet. There they were, sitting in a circle, and all of them were staring at baby Leo. He was standing on his head and whistling. Suddenly the Dingbats started making the strangest sound you have ever heard. It sounded just like people singing in church.

BUT NICER!

Minna was nearly in tears, but the others comforted her.

"He'll be happier now," they said and Minna dried her eyes and nodded.

Suddenly the Dingbats got up and off they went. Baby Leo and all the rest went galloping-galloping-galloping-galloping away with their funny-looking tails struck straight out behind them like broomsticks, roaring and bellowing and charging in and out among the trees with the harvest moon shining down on them like a great big smiley face.

And the baby milk wasn't wasted because the very next day Minna adopted a family of baby Hedgehogs who had lost their mother.

They were covered in fleas, of course, (all hedgehogs are) but they were very, very sweet.

HOODIES

Tom and Finch were out in the forest looking for Mugwumps and Minna was at home busy shampooing the baby Hedgehogs. It isn't easy to shampoo Hedgehogs, but it is perfectly possible provided one is patient and gentle, and Minna had plenty of patience and gentleness.

She had only just finished when she heard some strange sounds outside the treehouse and she listened anxiously. Nobody (except Beany) knew where they lived. So who on earth could it be? She heard someone cough... but then there was silence. After a long time someone knocked on the door.

"Who's there?" asked Minna nervously.

"I'm the Headmistress from the Village School," said a voice.

What a weird voice it was, thought Minna as she opened the door just a tiny crack and looked out. And what a weird-looking headmistress thought Minna. She had long dyed blonde hair down to her knees and thick,

thick spectacles that made her eyes look as big as ping-pong balls.

Behind her stood a row of children, and they were all exactly the same size, and they all stood perfectly still, and they all wore hoodies so Minna could only see their mouths.

"It's my class!" said the headmistress in a funny sort of voice. "Class 5B, and I'm taking them on a nature walk! To learn them all about the birds and the bees and, to tell you the gospel truth, deary, they hasn't had a drop of water for nearly half an hour, and them's suffering right badly with the hydrophobia!"

"Don't you mean dehydration?" asked Minna cautiously.

"That's what I just said!" said the headmistress. "Them's suffering right badly with hydrophobia and will soon become seriously ill and dropsical I wouldn't wonder!"

Minna stared at her.

"I beg you, little lady, I beg you to let us in for a drop of your sweet and lovely spring water!"

Minna hesitated. How on earth did the teacher know they had a spring Minna wondered?

Suddenly the teacher shoved Minna out of the way, and they all came storming in. She ripped off her blond wig and her glasses. Her black hair was braided in rat's tails and snakeskins! She spat on the floor and kicked the wig all round the room and jumped on it.

"Give us back our Rock-Diamonds," she yelled. "Those was our specials. And each and every one of dem's got a number! That's how special dem is!"

"I swear I don't know where they are!" Mina's voice shook with fear. "I swear it on my life!"

And this was true. She didn't know.

"All the worse for you, then!" screamed the Hill-Demon lady and the Hill-Demons went wild. They tipped the books off the bookshelves and the sugar out of the sugar bowl and the salt out of the salt cellar and the honey out of the honey pot and the jam out of the jam jar and the milk out of the milk jug and the eggs out of the egg box, and they ripped the clothes out of the cupboards and they yanked the curtains down and even ripped the wallpaper off the walls. (Minna had only put it up two days before!) They slashed the

cushions open with their razor-sharp daggers and ripped the pillows and quilts open with their razor-sharp teeth! There were feathers everywhere!

Then they all stood perfectly still and looked at the Hill-Demon lady and they still had their hoodies on and Minna could only see their mouths and their little pointy teeth. The Hill-Demon lady seemed to go into a trance. Then she looked at the floor and pointed. And her finger was all covered in crusty, sparkly rings.

"Pendunkulus Pendunkulo!" she hissed.

The demons went mad and began to rip up the floorboards. Soon there was a yell. One of the demons held up a box he had found. And the box had ROCK-DIAMONDS scrawled on it in Tom's big bold lettering. A mighty shout went up, and the one who had found it shook the box up and down and side to side... another one brought out a tin whistle and began to play and they all began to dance, and they danced up and down the walls, and they danced upside-down on the ceiling too, leaving filthy dirty footprints all over the clean white paint.

Suddenly the Hill-Demon lady clapped her hands together. She had put her wig back on, and her glasses too. The demons made a rush for the barrel where the spring water was kept and they drank the lot in fifteen seconds flat! Then they lined up behind the teacher and off they went. The one with the box of crystals clanked it up and down in time to their marching, and they all snaked away between the trees. The music became fainter and fainter in the distance until they were gone. When Tom and Finch got back, Minna was still standing with her back to the wall in a state of shock.

Tom and Finch stared at all the feathers. "Whatever have you been doing?" they asked. Minna went mad!

"What do you mean?" she shouted, tears of anger running down her face.

The others had never seen her so angry.

"It was your friends the Hill-Demons!" she shouted to Tom.

Tom and Finch looked really shocked. "The Hill-Demons!" they said. "Poor Minna! What did they do?"

"They took the Rock-Diamonds," Minna sobbed, and she pointed to the ripped-up floorboards. Minna and Tom hugged one another for comfort. But suddenly Finch collapsed on the floor. He was laughing so much he couldn't stand up. He tried to speak but he couldn't get his words out. It was a long time before Tom and Minna could understand what he was trying to say.

"They never found them. They never took them," he was saying, "'coz I switched them! I guessed where Tom hid them 'coz there was a mark on the floor... and so I switched them! I hid them up top where the Bats live!"

The others stared at him in amazement.

"What was in the box then?" Minna demanded.

"Sugar-lumps!" laughed Finch.

"You turnip!" said Tom admiringly.

"You genius," said Minna. And they both hugged him. Then they all fell about laughing. Soon all three were completely covered in feathers.

THE ECHO

For days on end Tom and Minna heaped praise on Finch, and Beany added his praise too; and for days on end Finch was as happy as a bee. They even got to hear about his cleverness in the village, where people began to talk about 'the boy who had tricked the Hill-Demons'.

But he was upset when Tom asked him to give him back the Rock-Diamonds. He had enjoyed thinking of the precious crystals hidden high up where the bats lived, in a secret place that only he knew about. It had given him a feeling of power.

He had given them back to Tom very, very reluctantly. Minna had suggested the three of them should share the crystals in future, and Tom, after much persuasion, had agreed to this. But it just wasn't the same. For days Finch went round with a long face, no matter what the others said, or did, to cheer him up.

Eventually there had been a blazing row and Finch stormed off, slamming the door behind him. Minna was worried and immediately opened it again.

"Where are you going?" she shouted.

"None of your business!" replied Finch rudely. But then he added: "I'm going to seek my fortune, if you must know."

"Where?" Minna shouted.

"In a place *I* know well," was all Finch would say.

Then he was gone.

Four or five miles away, on the other side of the river, there was an old wishing well that Beany had once shown him. In days gone by it had been famous and lots of people had gone there to make their wishes. There had been a proper path to follow then, but no one went there anymore. The path had long since disappeared and brambles and nettles had grown up all around. It was nearly dusk before Finch found the place.

The well was just as he remembered it only it looked more neglected now. Tiles had been blown off the little roof in a recent gale, the wooden handle and spindle were almost rotted away, and the bucket and chain were all rusty. Everything was covered with thick velvety moss.

The place looked sad and dingy and spooky. Finch sat down on the low mossy wall that surrounded the well and looked down. He could not see the bottom and he dropped a small stone into the inky blackness and counted very slowly: "One... two... three... four... five..." And then there was a 'plop' far, far down below. Finch looked down into the black depths. "Hello," he shouted.

"Hello," came the echo a moment later.

"I'm going to make a wish," shouted Finch.

"... make a wish," replied the echo.

"I'm going to make an important wish," shouted Finch.

"... make an important wish," replied the echo.

"My name is Finch, and I'm going to make my wish now!" shouted Finch.

"... you're going to make your wish now!" shouted the echo.

"That's funny," thought Finch to himself, and he leaned over a bit further and peered down the well. He thought he could see a queer-looking face peering up at him from far below, but he wasn't sure.

He cleared his throat. "In a moment I shall make my very important wish," shouted Finch.

"Oh, do get on with it!" shouted the echo.

Finch was so surprised he leaned over just a little bit further and slipped and fell. He turned over two or three times before he hit the water. Down he plunged to the bottom, and then up he bobbed to the surface, gasping for air. The water was not so very deep and, if he stood on tiptoe, he could stand with his head above the surface. It was almost dark, but Finch could see a little ledge just above water level. He tried to scramble onto it but something, or someone, grabbed his leg! It was something cold and slimy. It was as big as a man's arm and it squeezed his leg and then let go again.

Finch screamed! "What are you? WHO are you?"

"Oh, who can say what I am, or who?" replied a sad wishy-washy sort of voice.

"Are you the echo?" shouted Finch anxiously. He was scared stiff!

"Perhaps that's what I am, who can say," mumbled the voice. "Some people say that's what I am, but people say all sorts of things... and, anyway, no-one comes here any more."

Finch climbed onto the ledge and sat there shivering. There were lots of bowls and cups and dishes on the ledge, and every time he moved, one or two fell off into the water.

"Oh, don't do that, I beg you!" said the voice, "they are my treasures!"

"But what are you?" asked Finch again. "What shape are you? What do you look like?"

"Oh, who can say, and how?" replied the voice, "How can I know in this dark place?"

Finch tried to see the strange creature in the dark water, but he was not able to.

"Are these treasures all yours?" Finch asked after a bit. "They all seem to be a bit broken. This teapot doesn't have a spout."

"But it's Wedgwood," replied the creature indignantly. "And who needs a spout anyway. There's no tea here to pour, and who knows what tea is anyway?"

"Tea's what you drink at teatime," replied Finch. "And what's Wedgwood?" he asked after a little while.

"Everyone knows what Wedgwood is. It's what it's made of *and* how it's made," replied the creature earnestly. "And it soothes my poor skin. Anyone can tell Wedgwood by its lovely feel."

"How did you get here?" Finch asked next.

"I was put in here when men made the well," the creature replied. "That was 'undreds and 'undreds of years ago. And now you will be here for 'undreds and 'undreds of years to come, and live on the worms and crawlies that droppeth in of a nighttime."

Finch was silent for a while, thinking of the crawlies that he might have to eat.

"Tell me, what was your wish?" asked the creature at last.

"I wished for untold riches," replied Finch sadly, "for gold and silver and stuff, but then I slipped and down I came."

"Oh, what fathoms of foolery," said the creature sadly, "for you should have wished, firstly, for a way out of this dark place, but now it's too late, and you will be down here forever…"

Finch began to cry. What if Minna and Tom hadn't guessed where he was going, or if they couldn't find their way? What if it should rain, and the water got deeper and deeper?

"There is a mountain of gold and silver down below, and bronze and copper too," went on the creature after a while, "but I can't abide the touch nor feel of it, for it's all metallical, and its feel is painful to my poor skin. I let it lie there where it befell, year upon year."

Finch stopped crying and began to think of the untold riches down below.

"Some was cast down to the bottom when folk made their wishes, and some befell all unintended when folk leaned over a bit too far," went on the creature. "Oh, but you should hear the wailing and the rumpus when a necklace or a bejewelled pendant come rattling down all unintended! Oh my!"

"May I gather up the metallicals down below, Mr Echo?" Finch asked, after a while, in his politest voice.

"Oh, gather it all up to your heart's content," replied the echo. "There be an old bucket down there and you may befill it up to the brim with your gatherings."

To begin with, Finch tried to pick the precious bits and pieces up with his toes; but this was just too laborious and, eventually, he was forced to dive, time and again, to the bottom of the inky-black water, to feel about with his fingertips to try and fill the bucket up with all the things he found there. Once or twice he bumped into the Echo as he floundered about in the blackness. It was impossible to tell what shape the Echo was – it even seemed to *CHANGE* its shape.

But Finch wasn't scared of the poor creature any more. "Sorry," he would say, and the bubbles would carry the word up, up, and away into the darkness above.

By the time the bucket was filled to the brim, Finch was exhausted, and his teeth were chattering with the cold. As he dragged himself up, at last, onto the ledge to rest, he was overjoyed to hear, from far above, Minna and Tom urgently calling his name. It was a miracle that they found him as soon as they did. They hadn't known, at first, where on earth to begin their search... but suddenly (and both together) Minna and Tom had the same idea. For Finch had said, "I am going to a place that I know well!"

Was 'WELL' a clue???

Tom and Minna were soon sprinting through the forest in the direction of the Wishing Well. It was the only clue they had.

"Finch! Finch!" they shouted, both together, down into the inky darkness.

"Finch... Finch... Finch..." shouted the echo excitedly.

"Oh, Finch, are you all right?" shouted Minna.

"Oh, we're all right," shouted the echo.

"Yes, I'm all right, I suppose!" shouted Finch.

"What are you doing down there, you turnip?" shouted Tom.

"What are you doing up there you toadstool?" shouted the echo.

"I'm collecting my untold riches, but now I'm freezing!" shouted Finch, his teeth chattering with the cold.

"We're winding the chain down to you," shouted Tom.

"Oh, wind the chain down... and make good and sure a bucket be on the end of it!" shouted the echo.

The chain came clanking slowly down, and the bucket clanged and banged against the sides of the well as it came. Finch grabbed it and tipped his treasures in. "Pull it up!" he cried weakly – he was exhausted and very, very cold. The bucket went banging and clanking up again, and one or two bits fell out.

"What is it?" Tom and Minna shouted. "It's very heavy!"

"My untold riches," shouted Finch, shivering.

"It's gold and silver, and it's jewels and charms and keepsakes and brooches and bracelets and trinkets and necklaces and wristlets and medals and medallions and bangles and pendants and rings and amulets and bits and pieces of all manner of metallicals!" shouted the echo.

"Who on earth is that down there with you?" shouted Tom, as the bucket came banging down again.

"No one... well, a sort of someone. I'll tell you later!" shouted Finch, as he clambered into the bucket.

"No one. Well, a sort of someone, but who can say who or what?" called the echo.

Finch spun round and round as the bucket went up. He felt giddy and closed his eyes tight. Tom and Minna grabbed him the moment he was near the top and dragged him from the well. Tom peeled off his own dry clothes and made Finch get into them right away.

"Farewell Echo," called Finch, still shivering, into the inky blackness of the well.

"Fare thee well," came the echo.

"That's the queerest echo I ever heard," said Tom, looking at Finch, a puzzled expression on his face.

Finch said nothing. He was very cold and tired. He kept glancing at the bucket and longed to get home and tip its contents out onto the floor to see what he had got.

Tom and Minna carried the bucket between them – it weighed a ton – and they swung it to and fro as they trudged along through the bracken and brambles. Some of the riches fell out from time to time, but they didn't even stop to pick them up, they were just too tired.

Minna kept glancing at Finch. "What exactly is an echo?" she asked at last, as they stumbled along with their heavy load.

"Oh, who can say exactly what, or who?" replied Finch. He was very, very tired and still shivering.

The first thing they did when they got home was to get a good fire burning in the grate. And, as soon as his teeth had stopped chattering, Finch began to tell them all that had happened to him that day. But they were never able to decide exactly quite what an echo was.

BUNNY AND CLIVE

Sometimes when Tom, Minna and Finch were roaming about among the trees, they could hear the Dingbats squealing to each other in the dark heart of the forest, and this always made them feel a bit scared. How they hated that horrible sound!

But then the direction of the wind would suddenly change and they would hear other sounds: cars and lorries on the distant road for instance, or sounds from the village.

And so it was today: one minute they could hear cars and lorries, then suddenly the wind changed and they could hear music. They all heard it at the same time and looked at each other.

"Furze Fair!" they exclaimed simultaneously. They dashed back to the treehouse, grabbed the piggy bank and divided the contents into three. Tom and Finch dashed straight out again. "Coming with us, Minna?" they called as they sped off.

Minna shook her head. "I'll see you there," she said.

She watched her brothers disappear among the trees and smiled to herself; then she went up to her room. She sat in front of the mirror and stared at herself, and then she combed her hair with care. It had not been brushed or combed (or even washed) for ages, and was full of tangles and bits of grass. Next she parted it carefully in the middle. She stared at her reflection and began to pull faces. She tried out all sorts of expressions: wistful, soppy, jolly, sad, hard, mysterious... and decided that *mysterious* was the best.

Then she dressed herself in her cleanest clothes, put the fiddle carefully under her arm, and sprinted off in the direction of the music, holding it tight. It was Tom who had found the fiddle, early one morning, in the hedge. Some people thought it must have fallen from a gypsy caravan in the middle of the night; people in the village believed it to be a 'fairy fiddle'. It was very small, certainly, and made a lovely sound. Although it was really Tom's, it was Minna who cared for it, and it was she who played it, when her brothers were out of the way, or deep in the forest, with only the trees and birds to hear her.

The music grew louder and louder as she ran and when Minna scrambled through the hedge she saw the fair. There was a brass band playing a march, and a roundabout playing a waltz, and the two tunes were all mixed up together.

Suddenly she heard Beany's voice above all the rest. "Roll up! Roll up! Roll up!" he was yelling. "Pay your precious pennies and see the seventh wonder of the world. A poor old geezer who was born into this world without a topknot! A headless man, kiddies and gentlefolks! The only headless man in the whole wide world of wonders! Step this way, gentlefolk, step this way!"

Minna dashed past, hoping he wouldn't see her. Next she spotted Tom and Finch throwing wooden balls at the coconut shy. They were hurling the balls with such a spin that the coconuts were flying about all over the place. A man in a battered bowler hat was shouting at them angrily.

"That's cheating!" He was yelling. "How do you do it?"

Minna hurried on past and headed for the tent where the competitions were held.

"Do hurry up, dear," the lady in the hat said as Minna walked shyly in, "you're only just in time!"

Minna clutched her violin tightly, to make herself feel brave.

"What's your name, dear?" asked the lady.

Minna stood there looking about her: the tent was packed.

"Minna," she replied.

"Minna what?" asked the lady.

Minna nodded.

"Minna Watt?" asked the lady. "What an unusual name!"

Minna smiled.

"And what do you do?" asked the lady in the hat.

"I play the violin and sing and dance," Minna replied.

"Not all at once surely?" asked the lady with a laugh.

"Sometimes," said Minna slowly and precisely, putting on her mysterious, faraway expression. The lady in the hat gave a little giggle, and Minna sat down on the wooden bench with all the others. It was very hot in the tent, and some of the competitors were very boring. There was a boy who played the clarinet, a girl who played the accordion, some twins who played duets on the piano, and a very fat man who sang too loudly. It got hotter and hotter, and Minna dozed off once or twice.

When, at last, she was called up onto the platform, she felt very calm. First she played an Irish reel on the fiddle and everyone clapped loudly. Then she sang a very, very sad song about a young maiden who had lost her beloved in battle. She accompanied herself on the fiddle, and didn't make a single mistake.

At the end everyone clapped, cheered and whistled. Finally, she danced a jig, sang a comic song, and played the fiddle. *ALL AT THE SAME TIME!* The audience went mad. They clapped, cheered, shouted, whistled and stamped their feet on the wooden floor and they demanded an encore.

Minna ran round the back and hid. She had to be dragged out at the end of the afternoon to receive the first prize. The lady in the hat made a little speech, saying that she had never, in all her life, seen or heard anything quite so wonderful and extraordinary.

And then everyone started clapping and cheering all over again, while Minna stood on the platform with the competitors who had come second, third and fourth.

The first prize was a lovely silver cup with handles on either side; there was some beautiful curly writing engraved on the side. Everyone seemed to be staring at her. Did they want her to make a speech, or play some more music? Minna wasn't sure. She put the cup firmly under one arm and the fiddle under the other and then she made a dash towards the exit and the outside world, the applause still ringing in her ears.

As she charged out of the marquee, she was grabbed. A man grabbed one arm and a woman grabbed the other.

"Not so fast!" said the man.

"What's the hurry?" asked the woman.

"We'll take her to the van, Bunny," said the man.

"Alright, Clive," said the woman, and they dragged her off.

"Let me go!" shouted Minna.

Bunny and Clive pushed Minna into a dirty little bashed-up caravan, which was made of tin.

"We only want to help you," they said.

"I don't want your help. Give back my silver cup!" Minna shouted.

"Don't give it her Bunny," said Clive, "she'll only lose it."

"Make her sign a contract," said Bunny, "then she won't waste all her money.

"I haven't got any money!" shouted Minna.

"But she will have one day, won't she Bunny?" said Clive

"And we'll look after it for her, won't we Clive?" said Bunny.

Bunny and Clive went out and locked Minna up in the horrible smelly caravan. They got into a rusty little car that was parked next to it and Minna could hear them talking to each other.

"We'll get rich," said Bunny.

Clive laughed. "Very rich," he said. "*VERY* rich."

Minna shouted and beat on the window with her fists but people just smiled and waved at her. They thought she was waving to them. There was nothing in the caravan except some dirty cushions, some very stale chips all stuck together with grease and a torch. Minna carefully hid the torch in a safe place. She felt sure it would come in useful. Then she searched the caravan thoroughly to see if there was a way out, but there wasn't. Then she shouted and beat on the walls of the caravan again but everyone smiled and waved back at her.

Later that night, Bunny and Clive hitched their rusty little car to the caravan and started to tow it over the bumpy grass. Minna bumped about all over the place, she shouted and yelled but now there was no one to hear her and she began to sob.

In the weeks that followed, Bunny and Clive towed the caravan, with Minna in it, for hundreds and hundreds of miles. They went to fairs and circuses all over England and made Minna sing and dance and play her fiddle. Bunny and Clive kept all the money and hid it in a secret compartment somewhere in the car. They put a brass chain round her ankle to stop her running away, and told everyone it was gold.

"If it wasn't for that gold chain," they said. "She would fly away and come to harm. She's a fairy, that's what she is. A wild creature..."

If she sang or danced badly they gave her nothing to eat.

When she broke her fiddle they had it mended and punished her.

"No-one gets the better of us," they said.

Minna became more and more miserable and more and more desperate. "I'm getting sick of that girl," Minna heard Clive say one evening. "I think I'll sell her!"

"Who to, love?" asked Bunny.

"To Taffy McTavish's Travelling Menagerie," replied Clive.

"I've heard of Taffy McTavish," said Bunny, "He's famous."

Next day they started very early and drove

halfway up a mountain. They stopped when they came to a gigantic rock with a cave, half hidden, behind it. "Taffy said we should wait here," said Clive. So they waited all day and all the next night, too, but Taffy McTavish never showed up.

"I'm getting sick of this," said Clive, and they drove back the way they had come till they arrived back in the forest again. There was going to be a fair the next day and there were lots of caravans and cars and lorries there already. Bunny and Clive went to bed as soon as they arrived; they always slept in the car.

"You'd better give that girl something to eat, she hasn't eaten all day," said Bunny.

"You do it, love, my knee hurts," said Clive.

Minna was absolutely starving and she was freezing cold. She couldn't sleep. In the middle of the night she took the violin out from under the bed and began to play to keep herself company. She played until she was exhausted.

After she had put it away again she began to hear the strangest sounds from under the floor – scraping and scratching and scratching and scraping. "Who's there?" she called. The sounds stopped.

But then they started again. Bunny and Clive heard it too.

"There's someone breaking into the caravan, Clive," Bunny said. "Go and see who it is."

"Can't, love," said Clive. "It's my elbow, it hurts real bad."

"You said it was your knee," said Bunny.

"It *IS* my knee," said Clive, "but the pain's that bad it's spread from my flippin' knee into my flippin' elbow! Oh, the pain, the pain!"

"You're scared, aren't you?" asked Bunny.

"I ain't scared of nothing," shouted Clive.

Bunny got up and walked all round the caravan, but she couldn't see anything and went back to bed again.

"It's nothing," she said.

And then the sounds started again... scraping and scratching and scratching and scraping.

"Who's there?" Minna called nervously. She got her torch from its hiding place and knelt down and shone the bright light onto the floor where the sound was coming from. There was a thin, jagged gash in the tin floor, and Minna saw a tiny little spike, like a little sharp claw, cutting its way through the metal. Someone was cutting through the floor of the caravan from underneath *WITH A TIN OPENER!*

Before Minna could decide what to do, the floor collapsed. She fell sideways and rolled down and was grabbed by a score of hands. Someone clapped a hand over her mouth so she could not cry out. It was the Hill-Demons!

It was raining and the Hill-Demons half pulled her, half pushed and half carried her over the wet grass. They were running very, very fast. Clive and Bunny got out of the car and started shouting.

"Set the dogs on 'em!" Clive was yelling.

"We ain't got no dogs! You're so stupid sometimes!" yelled Bunny.

"We heard youse playin' yer fiddle, so we knowed it must be youse," said one of the Hill-Demons as they dashed along.

"So we thought we would rescue youse!" cried another excitedly.

"Here, have youse a sugar lump," said another, and dived his hand into his pocket and pulled out some dirty old sugar lumps.

THE HOLLOW TREE CHILDREN

Minna was so starving hungry she put them in her mouth without thinking and scrunched them up.

"We thought we would rescue youse 'coz, do you 'member? It was youse what gave we the sugar-lumps all them fortnights ago," said another.

"And we didn't even know, then, what sugar lumps was, and some of we called 'em 'suck-crystals' and some of us called 'em 'sugar-gems'!" said another.

"But now we knows what them really, really are and it's sugar lumps, sugar lumps, sugar lumps night till dawn and dawn till night," said another.

"And we jus' got to have 'em," explained another. "And everyday we goes out in Moonrocket and we goes to the sugar lump factories where they do make 'em, and we borrow sacks and sacks and sacks of sugar lumps... and we eats 'em all, each and every one."

"Go on. Have youse another sugar lump," said the first one.

They dragged Minna to a beaten-up rusty old

lorry with 'Moonrocket' and 'XZKQ' painted in red paint along the side of it, and they half lifted her, half shoved her and half yanked her up into it. The back was piled high with sacks and sacks and sacks of sugar lumps.

"Why is it called Moonrocket?" Minna asked, with her mouth full of sugar lumps.

A demon they called Weasel-Snout was at the controls and he just cackled as a reply. The engine started and they roared out onto the road. The tyres screeched. They were going very fast.

Almost immediately Minna heard a siren wailing and squealing behind them.

"What's that?" she asked nervously.

The Hill-Demons laughed. "It's the Scoobies," they laughed.

"Scoobies is police," one explained.

Minna looked back. A police car with a blue flashing light was chasing after them.

"Now us 'as got to ride," laughed Weasel-Snout. "'Coz them's got a Laser-gun, see? And Laser-light goes right through youse see? And melts youse up good and proper!"

He pressed a button marked 'DON'T PRESS' and there was a most horrible roaring sound.

Little stubby wings unfolded on either side of Moonrocket! The horrible roaring got louder. Black smoke and sparks poured out of the back. They were flying. "Now youse see why 'tis called Moonrocket," yelled Weasel-Snout.

The Hill-Demons laughed and shouted and whistled with excitement.

"'Tis a gun-powder rocket," they explained, "and it's all our own gunpowder, see, the gunpowder what we quarry-up from the gunpowder mine 'neath Gunpowder Hill?"

Thick black smoke came up through the floor and everyone fell about choking and laughing. Minna thought she was going to be sick. She went to the window and leaned out, gasping for air. How small everything looked down below.

Suddenly she saw the Treehouse. How little it looked — but there was no mistaking it. She called out to Weasel-Snout: "My tree! My treehouse! That's our tree down there. And there's the village. That's the crossroads."

Weasel-Snout yanked the steering wheel over, and Moonrocket turned sharply (causing several sacks of sugar lumps to fall off the side) and landed at the crossroads.

Because they were going a bit too fast they hit the signpost that said *To The Village* and snapped it clean off. How the Hill-Demons laughed. Minna leaped off quickly. Then they heard the police car. Minna could see the Laser-gun mounted on the roof, and as she sprinted off between the trees she thought she recognized Constable Dunstable at the wheel. And he looked very, very angry and was shouting something. With a roar and a rumble Moonrocket took off between the trees leaving a cloud of black smoke filled with little dancing sparklers of orange light.

How lovely it was to be home. It was after midnight and Tom and Finch (who were sharing a room again, for company) cried with happiness and hugged her tight. "But how thin you are, Minna," they kept saying. "Whatever did they do to you? Did they starve you, or what?"

They told Minna how they had searched the forest from end to end, and how Beany was going to every fair and circus in the land looking for Taffy McTavish's Travelling Menagerie. He had heard that Taffy McTavish had kidnapped her. Tom and Minna and Finch made an enormous fry-up, their biggest ever, and sat up nearly all night while Minna told of her horrible adventures.

Beany got back the next day, tired out, and was overjoyed to see them all piled up together in one bed.

YOUR LOVING
AUNTY MARY

Finch moved into his new room although it wasn't quite finished. He loved having a space of his own where Tom and Minna could not pester him. But, it was true, they could still yell at him from down below.

"It's your turn to wash the dishes," they would yell, and things like that, but at least he could pretend not to hear them. Beany hadn't made the window frames yet, but there were some quite large holes through the tree trunk and Finch could lean out of them and see far-away places.

Once the Owls came back to have a look at their old home, but they didn't stay long. One quick look — and then away they flew. Finch became more and more determined to find out where they had gone, and one day he followed after them and saw them glide into a hole at the top of a beech tree that had been struck by lightning years before.

One day, when the Owls were out, he climbed the beech tree and put his hand into the hole. There were two beautiful white eggs in the nest. They were almost round and Finch took one out very gently and stroked it against his cheek. It was lovely and warm and smooth.

Then he put it carefully back in the nest.

The middle of the nest was made of soft warm feathers, but the outside was just a jumble of twigs and leaves and even bits of paper. Finch took out one of the bits of paper and stared at it. One side was bright blue and glossy. It was a post-card. The bright blue bit was the sea and there were little boats on it. Half the card had been eaten away by beetles and snails, but most of the words on the back were easy to read. This is what it said:

Dear all,

It's so lovely and sunny here. Do come down soon while the lovely sunny weather lasts.

I'm dying to see you all,
Your Loving Aunty Mary.

Finch read the message over several times before he put it down his shirtfront next to his chest where it would be safe. Then he scrambled quickly down the tree. "I've got something important," he said before the others could say anything when he got home. Tom and Minna grabbed the card and read it over several times.

"How did it get here?" asked Minna at last. "If the postman brought it, why did he climb to the very top of the tree and shove it in a little tiny hole miles up in the air?"

"It wasn't that little," said Finch.

"And it doesn't even say for sure who it's to," said Tom. "The beetles seem to have eaten half of it."

"But you can see where our Loving Aunty Mary lives," said Finch. And it was true – she had written her address in neat and tiny writing along the top of the card: *Kerry Cottage, Station Parade, Findon-next-the-Sea.*

"We'll go tomorrow," said Tom, "while the lovely sunny weather lasts. I can't wait to see my loving Aunty Mary."

"*OUR* loving Aunty Mary. Not *YOUR* loving Aunty Mary," said Finch and Minna simultaneously.

Because the train station was on the other side of the forest, they were up before dawn. Beany was away and they left him a little note. When they got to the village train station they remembered they didn't have any tickets, but this didn't matter too much because Findon-next-the-Sea was not far from the village and they were in luck because it was Thursday – and Thursday was Market Day – and because on Market Day the station was packed. There were boxes of apples and sacks of potatoes and crates of chickens and bags of vegetables all over the place. Some were on the train already, and some were on the platform and some were stuck half in and half out of the train. There were farmers and farmer's wives everywhere, and lots of children and barking dogs.

The Guard was in a frenzy waiting to blow his whistle; he kept putting it in his mouth then taking it out again. "Come on now!" he kept shouting, "We're late enough as it is. Get this lot on will you. Mind your backs, will you. Mind your backs *PLEASE!*"

"Come here. If you don't come here this minute you'll get a good thumping," yelled a big fat farmer's wife carrying two gigantic polythene bags full of Spring Greens.

"We're coming, mum," yelled two little girls with long blond pigtails. "We're coming, Mum."

"We're coming, mummy, we're coming," shouted Tom and Minna and Finch pushing in between the farmer's wife and the Spring Greens.

"*DON'T LEAVE US BEHIND MOTHER*," screamed Finch at the top of his voice.

"She's not *YOUR* mummy," yelled the little girls angrily. "Get away!"

They were on the train at last. The door slammed, the whistle blew, and the train began to move. Tom and Minna and Finch dived under the seat. But, after a while, they crawled out and climbed onto the seat and looked out of the window. The trees whizzed by.

AN EVENING

OF MAGIC

QUIET PLEASE

"I never knew trees could go that fast," said Finch dreamily, and the others laughed at him.

"You know what I mean," he said.

They were sorry when they arrived at Findon and had to get out. The train ride had been most enjoyable. It was easy enough to find Station Road, but it was a long road and the day was hot.

They went up it and down it several times, and they asked lots of people, but there was no Kerry Cottage. The three of them sat down on the curb too miserable to speak.

And then a postman came clumping past with a post-bag on his back, and Tom called him over and showed him their postcard. The postman bumped his heavy bag down on the pavement.

"Bless my soul," he said. "That card must be years and years old. It's from Mary Maguire. I remember her. She went back to Ireland years ago. Her cottage isn't called Kerry Cottage anymore because the people who brought it changed its name. It's called Balmoral now!"

He picked his postbag up again and was about to go, but saw how miserable they all looked and he plonked it down again.

"Tell you what I'll do," he said suddenly. "My missus is called Mary and she loves kids. Perhaps she could be your loving Aunty Mary for a day or two!"

They stared at him.

"Come on!" he said.

The postman's wife, Mary, had grey curly hair and a jolly red face. She was all covered in flour and there was a lovely smell of baking in the house.

"Goodness gracious," she said. "I must be psychic. I just knew someone would be coming today, so I've made two cakes, a Lardy Cake and a Victoria Sponge. I hope you like cakes!"

She wiped her hands on her apron and patted her hair and then she wiped her specs. "That's better, now I can see you," she said and they felt at home right away.

Well, the days were lovely and sunny, just like it said on their picture post-card (which was ten years old) and Tom and Minna and

Finch played on the beach and swam in the sea every single day. They became as brown as berries and made lots of new friends and one day they won a competition for making the biggest and best sandcastle on the beach.

In the evenings they would make themselves some pocket money by collecting up bottles and cans and returning them to the cafe on the pier. Soon they were able to buy some lovely gifts for their new Aunty Mary and Uncle Bob. Beany too of course.

On the last evening of their holiday there was a big event on the pier. It was called "Family Nite" and anyone could go up on the stage and sing or dance or do a comic turn. Tom and Minna and Finch decided they would go and they dressed in their smartest clothes, which were brand new.

As so many people wanted to take part, they had to wait in a queue near the stage at the end of the pier. They could hear the sea swishing and swashing about down below. The stage had enormous red and gold curtains, and there were very bright lights that dazzled them and made them hot and sweaty. There were people who sang songs, or danced, and there were people who told stories and made jokes. Some of them were so boring they nearly nodded off standing in the queue...

But at last it was their turn.

They decided they would each do a magic trick and that Finch should do his first. The lights were so very bright that Finch couldn't even see the audience and to begin with he was a bit scared.

"Lordies and gentlefolk," he began. "I am going to do a magic trick with a watch, and I know you'll be truly scared when you see what I'm going to do. I need a really good watch made out of real gold if you please."

"Will my Rolex do?" asked a flashy looking man in the front row. Finch had never heard of a Rolex but he nodded eagerly.

"Hope he knows what he's doing..." said the man to the audience. He gave Finch the watch and the audience tittered.

Finch held up the watch. "I want everyone to have a good look at this perfectly normal watch," he said and then he wrapped it carefully in a red hanky. "Now I want you to watch what I'm going to do very, very carefully!" He put the red hanky with the watch in it on the floor.

Then he covered it with a cloth. Then he got a big hammer and hit it as hard as he could.

"Again! Again!" the audience roared."

Finch hit it again and again.

"Now," he said. "I want you all to watch very, very carefully. Then Finch lifted the cloth very slowly. "I'm going to show you something wonderful," he said softly. The red hanky was no longer red. It was YELLOW. Finch very, very carefully unfolded the yellow hanky and looked inside. Then his face went as red as a beetroot.

"What's happened, you idiot?" hissed Tom fiercely. Finch didn't say a word; he just stood there with his face all red.

The Rolex man began to climb on to the stage. "Let me have my watch," he said. The Rolex man looked at the watch Finch was holding. "That's not my watch!" he said. Finch didn't say anything.

"Is that my watch?" asked the Rolex man. Finch didn't say anything.

"Where's your mum, you flipping hooligan?" the man asked.

"Don't know," said Finch.

"Where's your dad?" the man asked, and his voice sounded all funny.

"Don't know," said Finch.

"I'm getting the Old Bill!" said the Rolex man and off he went.

Suddenly Tom had an idea. "And now we are going to do some REAL magic," he shouted. "Not conjuring tricks. REAL MAGIC. And we shall need YOUR help to make it work!"

Minna grabbed Finch. "Get in that box, you idiot," she hissed. "We are going to do that real magic trick that Beany taught us!"

They put Finch in the wooden box and put the lid on. Then they got a hammer and some nails and nailed him in.

"What you are going to see now is some really real magic," shouted Tom. "And I'm going to teach you some really real magic words. Alright?"

"*ALRIGHT!*" roared the audience.

Tom and Minna climbed on top of the box and held hands and began to dance about. They began to shout the magic words and the audience shouted them back. These are the magic words:

SHOUT AND YELL! YELL AND SHOUT!
STIR-ABOUT! TURN-ABOUT!

STOUT IS THIN AND THIN IS STOUT!
STIR-ABOUT! TURN-ABOUT!

SNOUT IS TAIL AND TAIL IS SNOUT!
STIR-ABOUT! TURN-ABOUT!

NOUT IS ALL AND ALL IS NOUT!
STIR-ABOUT! TURN-ABOUT!

OUT IS IN AND IN IS OUT!
STIR-ABOUT! TURN-ABOUT!

And suddenly there was Finch, dancing about on top of the box holding hands with Tom and Minna! The audience gasped.

"Oh! I thought you two would be in the box now instead of me!" said Finch.

"That's what I thought," said Minna.

"What's happened?" asked Tom.

An ear-splitting din was coming from the box – yelling and banging and shouting. The stage carpenters came running onto the stage with some tools and opened it up. The Rolex man was inside. He was all squashed up like a jack-in-a-box, and he was so squashed he couldn't get out. The stage carpenters dragged him out. His suit was all creased and he was red in the face with rage!

"Flipping hooligans!" he was yelling. "How did they get me in that flipping box, that's what I'd like to know! One minute I'm out in the road chatting to the Old Bill and next minute I'm banged up in that flipping box, the flipping hooligans!"

Tom and Minna and Finch looked bewildered. "How did that happen?" they asked each other.

And now a big fat man in a black shiny suit and a top hat was climbing up onto the stage, and some children were climbing up after him.

"It's me, the Fantabulous Fantino," the man roared. "You jus' gotta tell me 'ow you do dat fantabulous trick wid de magic box!" he roared.

"It really is the Fantabulous Fantino!" said some children excitedly. The one who's on the TV every Thursday!

"You jus' gotta tell me 'ow you do it, OK?" roared the Fantabulous Fantino again. "Then I jus' givva you de big monies, OK? I not talkin' peanuts, kiddies, I not talkin' pistachios. I talkin' the big smackeroonies... Look I show you!" He shoved his hand into his hip pocket and pulled out a big fat roll of £100 notes.

"Hey, that's real money that is," yelled the Rolex man, grabbing Mr Fantino's arm. "You can't go giving real money to those flipping hooligans. Look what they done to my flipping watch!"

And now a big fat lady in a shiny black dress and big shiny pretend-pearls came climbing up onto the stage.

"Don't you toucha my ole man," she was screaming. "No one toucha my ol' man 'cept for me, Mrs Fantino!"

She swung her handbag at the Rolex man and the Rolex man fell backwards into the orchestra pit. He landed bum-first in the big bass drum:

BARROOOOOOMPH!

The men and women in the orchestra pit went mad — especially the drummer. "You flipping hooligan!" he yelled. "Look what you've been and gone and done to my drum! That was my drum, that was! And now look at it!"

And he crashed the Rolex man's head between two big brass cymbals:

KRRASSSHHH!

Just like that!

KRRRASSSHHHHHHHHHH!!!...

He did it again!

"You leave my dad alone!" yelled a hunky teenager in a T-shirt with the word *TROUBLE* on the front in big red letters. He grabbed the drummer and threw him headfirst into a big enormous fish-tank full of piranhas.

Everyone was shouting now, and everyone was fighting everyone else.

"Come on," said Minna urgently. "It's time we were going back! Aunty Mary will be worried!"

The others agreed and they ran back along the darkened streets. How peaceful it was!

"Goodness me," Aunty Mary exclaimed. "Do you know what the time is? You're going home tomorrow and you will be tired out!"

Well, tomorrow came, and their new Aunty Mary put them on the train for home. They had got some proper luggage this time, which included their swimming costumes, beach towels and a few little luxuries for Beany (mainly Findon Rock and some Stilton Cheese). They also had tickets, which meant they enjoyed the ride home even more.

When they got home, the first thing they saw was Beany marching up and down outside the treehouse!

"Wherever have you lot been?" he demanded. "And what's all this baloney about going to stay with your Aunty Mary? You haven't GOT an Aunty Mary! I can't turn my back for five minutes without you lot vanishing away like smoke between the trees!"

GHOST HORSE

Tom, Minna and Finch didn't go to the village very often, not during the daytime anyway.

People used to stare at them and ask questions... questions like, 'Is it true you live in a tree?' or 'Is it true your granddad is a famous magician?' Things like that... but often they would go there when it got dark.

The place they liked best of all was the Thingmebob's garden: Thingmebob wasn't their real name of course, and their garden was just full of apple trees. Tom and Finch would climb about in the branches and throw the ripe apples down to Minna who would grab them, before they hit the ground, and put them carefully into the sack.

The Thingmebobs also had a lovely little pony whose name, funnily enough, was Apple.

Because the Thingmebobs didn't have any children, and because they spent their whole lives watching telly, Apple never, ever went out, used to get seriously bored. In fact she used to chew the top of her stable door out of frustration, so quite often, Tom, Minna and Finch would take Apple out, at nighttime, to gallop about in the forest. Of course, they would always bring her back before it got light, and they always, always brushed and combed her fur before they left.

The Thingmebobs just couldn't understand it. Mrs Thingmebob would stare, and stare, at Apple.

"I just don't understand it!" she would say, "looks like someone's been in the night again and... well ... groomed her all over!"

Mr Thingmebob would sigh.

"Oh, not again, dear!" he would say. "Must be those fairies again... or ghosties perhaps?"

"Well, there's SOMETHING funny going on!" Mrs Thingmebob would say.

One night the full moon was brighter than they had ever seen it before. It filled the whole forest with silver light.

"I know what, let's go to the heart of the forest!" said Tom.

"Yes! Yes!" the others said.

People from the village never, ever, went to the heart of the forest because they were scared. They believed that it was haunted by a ghost horse – a pure white stallion that had been there for hundreds and hundreds of years, ever since highwaymen had roamed there centuries before. The villagers named the ghost horse Pegasus after the fairy tale stallion who flew on huge silent snow-white wings over the forest trees.

To begin with they galloped along but then, after a bit, they cantered, and then trotted. Apple was a bit puffed. Finally they just ambled along, and then they stopped altogether. How quiet it was! And the moon was brighter than ever. Suddenly there was a scream!

"It's a rabbit!" yelled Tom, "some poor rabbit's got caught in a snare!"

The three of them charged off through the undergrowth... and there it was... caught in a snare. Minna quickly picked up the poor frightened creature and Finch pulled off the horrible snare and tossed it away into the brambles.

"Well, thank goodness we came tonight!" said Tom as the frightened rabbit scooted away into the night.

All they could hear now was owls... lots of owls... and there were lots of different kinds.

The kind they liked best were barn owls, the kind that go, "toowit towooo!"

One of them would call "toowit!" and then another would reply "towooo! Towooo!"

Finch decided to have a go. He cleared his throat: "toowit!" he cried out.

"towooo! towooo!" came the reply.

"Now I'm going to try!" said Minna. "Toowit!" she cried.

"Cooeee!!!" came a voice.

"That's funny!" said Finch. They all stared at each other. Minna cleared her throat again.

"Toowit!" she called.

"Coeee!!! Coeee!!! Coeee!!!" replied the mystery voice.

"That's funny!" said Tom. "Come on! Let's see who it is!"

Tom, Minna and Finch ploughed their way through the undergrowth pulling Apple along behind them.

"Cooeee!!! Coeee!!!" came the voice. She sounded quite close now. "Coeee!!!" And there they were – two of them.

"Hi!" said Tom, Minna and Finch to the two kids who stood there in the moonlight.

"Hi!" said the girl. "We're Allie and Kai!"...

"Yes! We're Kai and Allie!" said her younger brother.

"What on earth are you doing in the middle of the forest in the middle of the night?" asked Tom in amazement.

"Well, it's a long story!" replied Allie, with a sigh. "You see, someone gave us this... and..."

She picked up a big cardboard box. On the top of the box were the words *DO IT YOURSELF TENT!* And then, underneath, were the words *GO ON A DO-IT-YOURSELF-CAMPING-TRIP-THIS YEAR!* Underneath that there was a picture of a big orange tent with lots and lots of happy laughing children all round it.

"So we thought we would just... you know... do it!" said Allie. "Only everything wasn't quite right... the poles were either just too long or just too short... and..."

"And the strings were just a bit too short or a bit too long..." added Kai... he sighed.

"Does your Mum know where you are?" asked Minna.

"No! She'll be going mad!" said Allie anxiously. "In fact she'll have GONE mad by now!" added Kai.

"Come on! We'll have to get you back to the village real fast!" said Tom firmly.

"But how will you GET us there real fast?" Allie asked anxiously. "We've got a car!" yelled Finch.

"Where? Where?" cried Allie and Kai immediately.

"And a helicopter too!" yelled Minna getting carried away. They all laughed.

"Come on said Tom... we'll soon think of a way!"

"But first of all we must let Apple have a good drink. She needs one, I can tell," said Minna.

So they all ambled along till they got to the lake... which is right in the very middle of the forest. And the full moon was right in the very middle of the sky... so the water looked just like polished silver. And all the trees round the edge of the lake looked like silver too.

Apple waded deep into the still water and had a lovely long cool drink. How still it was...

and how quiet...even the owls had stopped their hooting.

But suddenly one of the children gasped. They all looked up. And there was a great white horse! There! On the other side of the lake! It was so still it looked like a statue!

"Pegasus!" whispered Finch in a scared whisper. Then Apple raised head and saw the great white horse standing there, and gave a delighted whinnie of greeting.

The great white horse didn't move. It just stood there like a statue. And then, suddenly, it neighed in reply. Ever so slowly, it began to swim towards them through the still deep water so that the moon's reflection, and all the stars too, became dancing patterns of silver light and, for a while, all they could see was its head. And then, suddenly, there it was. The two horses nuzzled each other and immediately became friends. The children clustered around them, talking to them and stroking them. Apple was little and cuddly.

Pegasus was enormous.

"We'll get you two home in milliseconds!" cried Tom excitedly. But it took quite some time to decide who was going to ride on Pegasus and who was going to ride on Apple. And then everyone kept changing their minds. But at last it was sorted. Allie and Kai wanted to ride on Apple, and the others leaped onto Pegasus's massive snow-white back that looked almost silver in the vivid moonlight. Both horses were soaking wet, but that just made it all more fun. They thundered along the forest tracks; some were quite narrow and twisted this way and that, and some were broad and straight because, two thousand years ago, they had been Roman roads. About half way, they had to cross a river. Apple splashed noisily through it, but Pegasus seemed to just glide from one side to the other. When they drew near to the village, Pegasus suddenly stopped. He would go no further. And then, suddenly, silently, he sped back to the forest.

Of course, the children went straight to Allie's house. All the lights were on. Allie's mum came to the door and yanked it open. Her eyes were all red, and she was still crying. She gave her children big hugs, and even hugged Tom, Minna and Finch, though all of them were wet through and muddy too.

"I went mad, I don't mind telling you!" Allie's mum kept saying, "Stark, staring mad! I phoned the police!

I phoned MI5! The BBC! Every one! I don't mind telling you! We've *ALL* being going mad, I don't mind telling you! Stark, staring, raving mad!!!" She thanked Tom, Minna and Finch over and over again for bringing them home safe and sound.

"Come on!" she said, "And now I'm going to fill you all up with something lovely!" She yanked open the fridge door and yanked out the biggest jug you've ever seen. "Juice!" she yelled, and began to fill some big shiny glasses, "it's *ORGANIC!!*" she cried in a special sort of voice – it was her favourite word.

"What's organic mean?" Finch whispered to Minna.

"It means really special!" Minna whispered back.

"Hope it don't mean weird!" whispered Finch.

But it was quite nice.

After that they took Apple home.

"Tell me – did you notice anything a bit... er... funny, when we crossed that river?" asked Tom suddenly.

Minna and Finch glanced at each other quickly.

"Do you mean... er... real funny?" Minna asked.

"Do you mean... when we... sort of crossed the river?" Finch asked.

All three exchanged glances.

Tom looked serious. "Yes... when we, crossed the river, and sort of... well..."

"Sort of... flew?" said Finch.

"Sort of... floated?" said Minna.

Tom sighed. "Look..." he said. "Let's not tell Beany... not right away any way, 'coz he might think we..."

"Sort of ...dreamed it...?" they all said.

Next morning Mrs Thingmebob had a shock when she went to give Apple some hay. She stared in amazement.

"Darling!" she shouted, for Mr Thingmebob was still in bed.

"What is it dearest?" he replied grumpily.

"Just come and have a look for yourself!" yelled Mrs Thingmebob.

Mr Thingmebob came to have a look.

"Have those fairies, or ghosties or whatever they are, paid us another visit?" he asked grumpily.

"Well! What do *YOU* think?" she replied, "just look at her coat – all brushed and combed. And her mane and her tail too!" she added.

Mr Thingmebob stared. "And her hooves too..." he added blankly. "All cleaned and polished?"

"You have to agree? It's a bit... odd? Isn't it?" demanded Mrs Thingmebob.

"There's only one word for it!" said Mr Thingmebob with a frown. "It's CREEPY!"

A MAGIC SPELL

Tom, Minna and Finch missed being by the sea, particularly since they had their smart new swimming costumes to wear. But luckily there was a lake that was not too far from where they lived. It was a big lake and the water was very deep, yet crystal clear. A little river fed the lake: it ran in at one end and out the other. In the middle of the lake was an island.

After their holiday they went to the lake nearly every day. There was a little sandy beach but hardly anyone ever went there... just a few fishermen, who stood all day long holding their fishing rods and gazing across the water.

Tom and Finch caught plenty of fish but they were mainly little ones. Minna felt sorry for the fish but she collected freshwater mussels, which are very good to eat (if cooked properly) and sometimes (if you are lucky) they might contain a tiny little pearl. Minna found several small pearls and hoped eventually to collect enough to make a necklace or, at least, a bracelet.

One day, swimming about in the lovely clear water where it was really deep, they caught sight of a sunken canoe. It had turned over and was lying upside down in the waterweed. They dived down again and again hoping to free it, but the waterweed held it tight and it would not budge. The next day they returned with Beany.

Beany, strange to say, had always been scared of water and he was determined to keep a safe distance from the lake.

"I was swallowed by a whale when I was a lad," he used to say. "You won't catch me going in the water!"

"But if you were really swallowed by a whale, you wouldn't be here today," people would say to him.

"HALF swallowed then!" he would reply obstinately.

Beany promised to raise the canoe from the bottom of the lake using one of his spells on condition that he did not have to get wet,

and he asked to be shown exactly where it lay. Tom was able to show where it was by throwing little stones into the water. Beany sat on a rock and closed his eyes.

After what seemed a very long time, he opened them again and pointed at the water. At first there was nothing... but suddenly there was a little ripple... and then another one... and then another one. There was something there, floating on the surface of the lake, and a great cheer went up.

"It's not very big, is it?" said Minna.

Tom and Finch swam out as fast as they could to have a look. And what they found, floating there, was an old boot.

They were all very disappointed, Beany most of all. He was inclined to blame Tom for showing him the wrong place, and he went stomping off to his hideaway claiming he had to do some repairs to the roof. It was an excuse actually, because he was fed up that yet another of his spells hadn't worked quite as intended.

Tom, however, had noticed something very important. The boot had a BUBBLE in it, and this had given him an idea. He thought about bubbles when he went to bed that night, and he dreamed about boots, bubbles and boats.

Next morning, he got up early and dashed down to the village and returned with a length of green garden hose, which he had borrowed from someone's garden without telling them. It wasn't very new, but it was very LONG.

The three of them carried it quickly down to the lake. Tom dived right down to the bottom and put one end of the hose under the canoe; then they took it in turn blowing down it.

The bubbles rose up inside the canoe and became a mega-bubble. The canoe got lighter and lighter in the water and suddenly the waterweed was swept away and up it came with a rush!

Tom, Minna and Finch grabbed it excitedly and dragged their prize ashore. After giving their new canoe a good clean they made some paddles and later they added a little sail. They soon learned how to sail the canoe and decided to name it Mayflower.

One of the first places they went to in their new boat was the island. They were a bit scared the first time they went, as it was much further than they thought, but as they leaped ashore, they were enchanted by it.

The island was everything that they had imagined. The water was warm and shallow and full of fish and freshwater mussels. Some campers must have been there before them because they found an old, bent frying pan. Now they could cook the fish and mussels they had caught over a fire and eat them with campfire bread known as 'Damper'.

On one of their visits, Finch discovered an old sail lying in the shallow water. It was torn, and that was probably the reason it had been thrown away. Perhaps it had come from a yacht called Mallard, for it had Mallard stencilled on it in green letters. It seemed a shame to waste it, and they hung it up to dry. Next they leaned some poles together and tied them at the top. And, after that, they wound the sail round and round the poles and made a tepee.

Of course, they were careful to make it among the trees and brambles where no one would see it. It was very warm and snug inside the tepee and, although they were not quite brave enough, yet, to sleep in it by themselves, they decided to leave it there for next time.

After a long discussion inside the tepee they decided to name the island Mallard Island.

After that Tom, Minna and Finch talked about Mayflower and Mallard Island all the time. Beany pretended not to listen, but secretly he longed to visit the island, which he had so often seen from far away. Sometimes he would sneak down to the water's edge to see if he could see Mayflower. But he couldn't... it was too well camouflaged.

Then he would gaze at the island... how beautiful it looked! Beany sighed and went on his way.

ANOTHER MAGIC SPELL

One fine day, towards the end of summer, Minna said: "You know we really should ask Beany out in Mayflower one day. He's never even seen it yet and he's never been to Mallard Island."

"He'd never come!" said Finch. "He'd say he was half-swallowed by a whale when he was a lad, and all that stuff."

"We could bribe him, I suppose," said Tom. "We might catch a carp, or something, and promise him a fish supper... you know how much he loves a fish supper!"

When Minna invited him he pulled a face.

"And get a soaking, I suppose," said he grimly, "like that time when I was a lad and got swallowed by that blinking whale!"

"Half swallowed," Minna reminded him. "And anyway," she added. "I promise you that you won't even get your feet wet!"

"I'll think about it," said Beany. "Yes, I'll definitely think about it," he added and

stared up at the ceiling and began to hum a little tune.

In fact, he had already made up his mind.

Next day, Tom and Finch began to get their fishing lines ready, but this took a long time as they didn't have proper reels and their lines were always in a tangle. But this gave Minna enough time to get her cooking things together and put them in the boat.

At last they were ready to go. Beany got in first, very slowly, and seated himself with care up at the front end of the boat (the bows) which he thought would probably be the safest part. He was scared stiff. The others leaped lightly aboard, the breeze filled the little sail that they had made and they began to move.

Tom and Finch threw their fishing lines out into the clear deep water. Beany gazed across at the island, wishing he were there already. Swifts and swallows darted low over the lake greedily snapping up the flies and gnats. How peaceful it was! By the time they were half way there Tom and Finch were beginning to get worried. They weren't catching any fish at all.

"No fish, no dinner!" said Beany sadly.

"They're just not biting, that's the problem!" Finch muttered.

"Gnats are though," sighed Beany, scratching his head. "Gnats are biting a treat."

So, there they were, sailing slowly, ever so slowly, towards the island, and they were quite close now, and then Finch caught a stickleback. "It's a tiddler, I'll chuck it back," he said.

Tom and Minna and Finch were all leaning over the side gazing down into the crystal depths. "There's loads of fish down there," they said. "Big ones too!"

"Sometimes I begin to wonder if you can really catch fish at all!" said Beany unwisely.

"What do you mean? We're always catching fish. You've seen us," Tom and Finch replied angrily.

"Oh I've seen you catch tiddlers," said Beany to wind them up, "but never anything bigger than a tadpole that I can remember!"

"And I don't believe you can do real spells," said Finch defiantly. "Not big ones anyway... just tiddlers... and even then they go wonky."

Beany stretched his legs and stared up at the sky above. "Why, I know a spell," he boasted. "Yes, I know a spell that would call up the biggest fish in the lake. There, Imagine that. The biggest fish in the whole lake. Think of that!"

"Beany, dear Beany," began Minna in her most wheedling voice. "Please call up your big fish. Or we shall all go to bed hungry tonight."

But Beany shook his head. "What if it were to be be a forty-pound pike?" he asked. "Would those brothers of yours be able to handle it? What do you think?"

"We've landed forty-pounders enough times," they scoffed.

"Please," begged Minna.

Beany sighed. "I'll think about it," said he as he began to get ready to do the spell. "I shall need your help," he added. "All you've got to do is hum. Mmmmmmmmmmmmmmmm," he hummed and stopped to catch his breath. "Mmmmmmmmmmmmmmmmmmmmmmmm... just like that... oh yes... and close your eyes while you're doing it!"

So they closed their eyes and hummed while Beany dipped his finger in the water and spoke some magic words. The humming made them feel drowsy and they were almost asleep when Beany told them they should stop. Beany looked a bit sleepy too. They all looked over the side into the clear water.

"Have a look," Beany said triumphantly.

"All the tiddlers have gone!" said Tom and Minna and Finch.

"Scared, see," said Beany "They've probably seen the big one coming!"

"But the big ones are whizzing off too!" said Tom.

"A pike more than likely, just like I said!" said Beany.

"But now the pikes are whizzing off too!" said Finch.

"Oh lor!" whispered Beany miserably, screwing himself up into a ball, there's something big comin' up!"

The lake itself seemed to heave a sigh. First the water went up a little... and then it went down a little. And then Tom, Minna and Finch let out a terrifying scream! They had all seen it whizzing up towards them! A monster-fish with huge staring eyes! It's huge mouth, fringed with long sharp teeth, was wide open!

CRASH! CRUNCH!! CRACK!!!

It grabbed the boat and shook it. Then it tossed it up in the air. Tom and Minna and Finch and Beany went up in the air too. Next thing they knew they were in the water. Luckily they were very near the island and Tom, Minna and Finch were ashore in a moment; but then they had to go back for Beany who couldn't swim. They pulled him and pushed him to the shore and yanked him and dragged him up the little beach and onto the dry grass.

So there they all sat, shivering with fright and staring at the water. Mayflower was upside-down but still afloat. There was no sign of the monster-fish. It had returned to the bottom of the lake.

Beany was the first to speak. "But you promised me I wouldn't get my feet wet," he said at last. "And look at me now: I'm drownded!" He looked at Minna with his big sorrowful eyes.

For a moment no one said anything, but then they all fell about laughing. Even Beany laughed in the end, though not quite so loudly (or quite so long) as the others.

RED SKY AT NIGHT

That first night on Mallard Island Beany went to bed really early, as he wanted to hang his clothes out to dry as soon as possible after the "shipwreck", as he called it.

"Blow me if I wasn't half-swallowed a second time," he kept grumbling. "Probably that same confounded whale having another go!"

"It was a fish," they reminded him, "and, anyway, it didn't get you."

"Jolly nearly," he replied. "Anyhow, I think I'll sleep in the igloo."

"Tepee!" Minna corrected him.

"Tepee, then!" he replied and went to bed.

Tom and Minna and Finch slept out, as they often did when the weather was fine. There was a little hill in the middle of the island and, from the top of it, by the silver light of the moon, they could see nearly the whole lake.

They decided to call it Lookout Hill. The turf there was dry and springy, and the grass was soft and had a lovely smell. They spread their blankets down on the warm ground in great contentment.

"Who needs a tent when they've got the sky above them?" asked Tom happily.

"And who needs a campfire when they've got the moon for company?" asked Minna.

"Who needs a blanket when they've got the stars to keep them warm?" yawned Finch.

"But you've got a blanket anyway," Tom reminded him.

"But I don't actually *NEED* it," replied Finch sleepily.

"Give it to me then," said Minna, making a grab for it.

"No!" said Finch firmly, holding it tight.

The three lay there contentedly staring up at the summer sky.

Earlier, swifts and swallows had sped low over the lake snapping up the flies, but they had all gone now and there were bats to watch instead. They flittered about, squeaking in their high-pitched reedy voices, snapping

up the moths and midges. There was always something to look at and, every time they were ready for sleep, something would happen and they would be wide awake again.

A shooting star whizzed across the sky.

Then another.

And then an owl flew low over their heads on silent wings. It gave a screech, when it saw them, and they were all scared for a moment.

And then some swans flew across the moon. Then, suddenly, a big flock of geese flew down from the sky. They honked anxiously to each other before landing, with a flurry, on the water.

"Shut up!" Finch yelled, and Tom and Minna got the giggles.

At last they fell asleep.

They were still asleep when Beany set out to explore the island next morning. He laughed to see them lying there, rolled up under their blankets like dormice. Beany was enchanted by the island and explored it thoroughly from side to side and end to end. He found all kinds of spices and herbs, and brought them back to the camp. There were herbs to cure coughs and colds and spots and all kinds of injuries and illnesses, and spices for Minna who was the chief cook.

Tom and Minna and Finch spent most of their time over the next few days splashing about in the water and catching fish. There was nothing to eat on the island except for fish, and they took it in turns to cook dinner in the evening, but Minna was voted the best cook and, on their last evening on the island, she cooked Stargazey Pie, which is a Cornish pie made from seven different kinds of fish.

"I'm beginning to get a bit tired of fish pie," sighed Finch, as they all sat round the fire that evening.

"I'm not," said Beany, "you can't beat fish-pie. And, anyway, fish is the best food in all the world. Everyone in the world knows that! Some folk calls it 'brain food'. Did you know that? And that's because it feeds your brain, and makes you smarter every single time you have it."

"Is that true?" asked Tom doubtfully.

Beany nodded. "And now I'm going to tell you something," he said mysteriously. "I was on a train once, oh, years ago it was, and there I was sitting opposite a most learned

man... a scholar for sure. And, when it was lunchtime, he took out this little lunchbox. A lovely thing it was, made like a little casket. And when he opened the lid, it played a little tune. I was entranced by it!

"Well, he opens the lid, and, hey presto, inside there was some lovely crusty bread and a tasty-looking fish, and he gets out a knife and fork and he cuts off the head, and he cuts off the tail, and begins to eat his dinner. I was ravenous, and kept on staring at him. 'Fish is the best food in all the world,' says the scholar with his mouth full when he saw me staring at him. 'It's really, really delicious,' he said, 'and it's really, really good for you... and it's good for the brain in particular. That's why some call it 'brain food'!"

"Is that a fact?" says I.

"The scholar nods his head. 'Why,' says he, 'I have three fine sons, and, do you know, my wife and I used to give them fresh fish for dinner every single day when they were little. And now they're grown up and, guess what. One is a surgeon, one is an atomic scientist and one is a cosmologist!'

"Well, I was lost in admiration when I heard this, but I was hungry, too, and I may have mentioned that I had had no dinner that day. 'I'll tell you what I'll do,' says the kindly scholar. 'Just give me £1 exactly, and I'll let you have the head and the tail, for they are the tastiest bits of all, and I was saving them till last!' Well my tummy was rumbling by then, and I was glad enough to give him my £1, which was all the money I had, incidentally.

"So the scholar let me have the head and the tail, and they were very delicious, I must say, even though there is precious little meat on the head of a fish... and less still on the tail. 'That was lovely,' said I, a bit disappointed like. I had finished my portion, you see, but he was still chomping away. 'Please would you be so very kind as to tell me what kind of tasty fish that was,' says I, 'and where can I can get such a delicious delicacy for meself?' 'This is a very special fish indeed,' replied the scholar, with his mouth full, 'and I purchased it for £1 exactly!'

"'Hold on a minute!' says I, after a moment. 'You say it cost you £1 exactly... but I gave you £1 for just the head and the tail of it and there was scarcely a scrap of meat on either!' Well, the kindly scholar looks me in the eye and beams. 'There you are!' says he, 'it's working already! Just two or three little mouthfuls and your brain is working as never before!'"

Beany laughed so much he rolled over on the grass and couldn't stop. But Tom and Minna and Finch looked angry.

"That makes you look really stupid!" said Tom, at last.

"No, it doesn't," insisted Beany. "I was only young at the time, anyway."

"That doesn't matter," said Finch sternly. "It still makes you look really dumb!"

Suddenly Beany stopped laughing. "Crikes," he said, "I wish I had me paints!"

The others turned to look. It was the loveliest sunset they had ever seen. The sky was red and crimson and scarlet and gold and they stared at it, watching the colours changing from moment to moment.

"Red sky at night, shepherds delight," said Minna happily, covering the embers with a turf so as to keep the fire alive till the next morning.

"Red sky at night, shepherds take fright, is what my old mammy always used to say," said Beany, puffing at his pipe.

Finch looked puzzled. "Which one is right?" he asked.

"We shall have to see," said Beany. "But I think we should all sleep in the tepee tonight. Just to be on the safe side."

It was a bit of a squeeze in the tepee, and it was a bit wobbly because it only had one guy-rope as all the rest had been used to make clothes lines and fishing lines. Tom, Minna and Finch were asleep in a moment – they had been sleeping out all week under the stars and felt extra especially snug under the canvas.

But Beany just couldn't relax. He kept hearing his mammy's voice. "Shepherds take fright, Beany, just remember that!" he heard her say in his ear as he lay there in the dark. And then the wind began to blow!

RED SKY IN THE MORNING

The gusts of wind became stronger and stronger and the leaves in the treetops hissed like rushing water. Soon the ripples on the lake turned into waves and Beany could hear them crashing on the shore only a short distance from the tepee. And then the tepee began to shake! Beany lay there under his blanket with just his nose poking out.

Suddenly he heard voices, loud horrible voices shouting and swearing nearby... and then there was a horrible shout just outside the tepee, only a few inches from his ear! Beany sat up, rigid with fright.

"Come out of your wigwam you heathens!" the horrible voice cried, and Beany nearly jumped out of his skin.

"Come out straight away, or we'll come in and get you!" cried another voice as horrible as the first.

Beany scrambled out of the tepee on all fours and was immediately grabbed by his collar and yanked up in the air by the pirate chief. Beany knew he was a pirate chief because he was wearing an enormous sea captain's hat with the skull and crossbones emblazoned on the front of it. He had only got one eye and one ear. Beside him, on one side, stood a man with only one leg and, on the other side, a man with only one arm, and the man with only one arm had also lost his nose. You could see where it had been though.

Behind them, Beany could see a great three-masted pirate ship, its black sails flapping and banging about in the wind. Beany stared at it in amazement. He couldn't believe his eyes.

"Show us the channel, you heathen!" bawled the pirate chief in Beany's face. "We've been around and around this puddle all night long, caught like a lobster in a pot. Show us the channel you old barnacle!"

Then he dumped Beany down on the ground with a bump.

"What channel?" asked Beany, rubbing his eyes in disbelief.

"Why the channel out of this puddle and back to the sea, you barnacle!" roared the pirate-chief.

"Back to the sea?" Beany mumbled, staring at the great black ship. It was the biggest he had ever seen... and there it was... floundering about on the beach... a bit tilted over... with some of its black sails still flapping and crashing about in the wind. The decks and the rigging were swarming with pirates. They were all shouting and swearing at each other and pulling on ropes and reefing down the sails and charging about all over the place.

"There's no channel," mumbled Beany, at last. "You can't get to the sea from here. There's just a bit of a stream that runs in and another one that runs out. And that's all."

"Oh, there's a way in all right and there's a way out!" bellowed the pirate chief. "Bug-eyes sailed us in on the night watch, but he was as skewbald as an albatross he was, and has no remembrance of it! Tell us where it be... or we'll... or we'll..."

"Shall we cutlass him up, Skip?" asked the man with only one leg.

"Shall we, shall we?" begged the man with only one arm and no nose. The pirate-chief considered this for a moment. "Put your blades away," he said at last. "Go in the wigwam and bring without all that is within!"

"You shall not enter!" Beany roared, rushing forward, but the one-legged man grabbed him and tied him roughly to a tree while the one-armed man charged into the tepee.

"What have we got?" yelled the pirate chief. "Any confectionery?"

"Can't see no confectionery, Skip!" replied the one-armed man.

"Any cordials?" roared the pirate chief.

"Can't see no cordials, Skip, "but there be three kiddies asleep in their blankets."

"Bring them without!" yelled the pirate chief.

"You shall not touch them!" Beany cried, but he could not free himself from the ropes that bound him, and other pirates came running up and dived into the tepee.

Tom and Finch and Minna fought like demons. They kicked and punched and scratched and bit. But the pirates threw them over their shoulders, like sacks of potatoes, and carried them out. The pirate chief laughed when he saw them. "They'll make useful look-out boys!" he said.

"But one of 'em looks like a girl!" said the pirate with only one arm and no nose, "her hair be all long and curly!"

"Then she'll cook and she'll serve!" cried the pirate chief with a laugh. At once, all the ruffians broke into song, and this is the song they sang:

She'll make us hot dinners.
It's what we deserve
And she'll cook and she'll bake
And she'll carry and serve!

And next came the chorus:

Aye, she'll make us hot dinners,
As hot as can be
Else her bones will bleach white
On the bed of the sea!

And then they all laughed.

"Let the bairns go!" roared Beany struggling with the ropes that held him, but the pirate chief laughed and laughed, showing all his big horrible yellow teeth.

"Take the bairns aboard!" he yelled to his men.

"Let them go and I'll show you the channel!" roared Beany suddenly.

"But you said there was no channel, you old barnacle!" shouted the pirate chief angrily, bits of spit coming out of his mouth with every word.

"I was joking you, 'coz of course there's a way out, and I've knowed it since I were a lad!" roared Beany, struggling with the ropes.

The pirate chief looked at him with his one eye.

"Show me," he said, at last.

"Free me first," Beany demanded. "Then I'll show you."

The pirate chief cut through the knots with one swish of his cutlass and, together, they walked down to the water's edge.

"Show me!" said the pirate chief again.

Beany pointed out across the water.

"See against the sky?" he said. "See over to the east, where it's getting light?"

The pirate chief looked. "See the two mighty elms?" Beany asked.

The pirate chief nodded.

"You must sail between them," said Beany.

The pirate chief stared across the water, and the wind whistled and roared. "They're very close together," he said, staring at Beany with his one eye.

"They're close together, but the water between them is deep and the channel is straight and true," said Beany.

The pirate chief looked across the water. Then he laughed and slapped his thigh. "All aboard!" he roared at the top of his lungs.

"Wind's goin' about, and the channel is clear to see! All aboard, lads, all aboard!"

"Aye aye, Skip!" roared the pirates, all together.

"Give me back the bairns like you said!" bellowed Beany furiously.

But the pirate chief laughed.

"I was joking you!" he said, and laughed again. The pirates were scrambling back onto the boat now, and Beany could see Tom and Minna and Finch being carried aboard.

"I'm comin' to get you!" roared Beany, and he began to run. He ran as he'd never run since he was a young lad. He galloped along like a young Billy goat.

"I'm comin'!" he yelled, and as the pirate chief turned, Beany leapt high in the air and head-butted the pirate chief in the middle of his big horrible beer belly.

"Arghhhhhhhhhhhhhhhhhhhhhhhhhh!!!" groaned the pirate chief, and down they went, the two of them, into the shallow water at the edge of the lake.

Beany was on top, but a hundred hands grabbed hold of him and pulled him this way and that. "Lemme go you barnacles!" he roared. But it was Finch and Tom who were shaking him. "What's all this stuff about barnacles?" they kept asking. "Are you having a bad dream or something?"

Beany opened his eyes. "Oh lor!" he said, "That were the most stupidest dream I ever had in me whole life!"

"The tepee's fallen over," said Tom. It was true. There should have been at least three guy ropes but they only had one. All the others had been used for fishing lines.

"Haul down the halyard you barnacles!" yelled Beany, but then he remembered where he was. "Sorry!" he mumbled.

It was nearly dawn so they decided to roll the tepee up and light the campfire for breakfast. The eastern sky was all lit up with red and amber and gold.

"Wish I had my paints!" said Beany, gazing at the lovely colours.

"Red sky in the morning, a shepherd's warning," said Minna, blowing the campfire till it flared into life.

"Red sky in the morning, a fine day is dawning. That's what my old mammy used to say!" said Beany.

"You had better tell us about that dream you had," said Tom as he put the kettle on the fire.

"Oh lor," said Beany shaking his head. "It was just too stupid to tell." But they kept on and on and on at him till he gave in at last.

"Oh, alright," he said, and he sighed and began to light his pipe from the fire.

"Well, there I was in the tepee, and the wind was gettin' stronger and stronger by the minute. Suddenly there was a horrible shout. It was really horrible, I can tell you. 'Come out of your wigwam you heathens!' shouted this horrible voice. 'Come out straight or we'll chop you up!' shouted another horrible voice. It made my hair stand on end, it really did. Well I scrambled outside and there was all these pirates charging about all over the place. There were hundreds of 'em. And there was this great big enormous sailing ship floundering about on the beach. Well, this great big fella, the one with only one eye, grabbed hold of me and yanked me clean up in the air, just like I was a little dog or something. 'Show us the channel!' he roared,

"'Show us the channel, or we'll chop you up into hundreds and hundreds of little tiny pieces...' Those were his very words! Into hundreds and hundreds and hundreds and hundreds of little tiny weenie pieces!"

Beany told them the whole story, just as I've told it to you. When he finished, it was time to go home.

Tom had mended the teeth holes in the boat with resin from a fir-tree.

"It's as good as new," said Minna.

"It's better than new 'cos it's got battle scars on it now," said Finch.

They piled their few belongings into the bows – all the herbs and spices that Beany had collected, Minna's shells and pearls, and the new fishing rods that Tom and Finch had made – and then in they got.

"Hope we're not shipwrecked this time," said Beany to himself. They put the sail up and waved goodbye to Mallard Island and Minna blew it a kiss. As there was not much of a wind, Tom wanted to use the paddles to speed them up, but Beany begged him not to. "The sound of the paddles might waken that great beasty," he said. "Let it slumber on, and dream its wicked dreams."

They were over half way now. How still it was.

"Just think" said Beany suddenly, "the water's over a hundred feet deep here! Over one hundred feet, just think of that! Suppose we should suddenly sink! We'd all be drownded! Every single one of us! And there'd be no book!"

"Drowned, not drownded," said Minna. And then she suddenly looked up.

"What book?" she said sharply.

Beany wished he hadn't said anything, but they all looked at him.

"What book?" Minna asked again.

"Where is the book?" Tom asked.

"*THIS* book," said Beany.

"What do you mean *THIS* book?" they asked, staring at him.

"*THIS* one said Beany. "The one we're all *IN*!"

"I don't get it!" said Finch.

"Who put us in it?" asked Tom.

"Is it something to do with your magic?" asked Minna. "Is it one of your magic spells?"

Beany looked down at his feet. "Who can say?" he said modestly. He hoped there wouldn't be any more questions and, at that very moment, Mayflower ran gently onto the muddy beach at the edge of the forest. There were the fishermen, holding their rods and gazing silently across the still water, and behind them the great forest trees, majestic and beautiful in the summer sunshine.

"Hooray! We're back!" they all yelled, and leaped ashore.

Soon they were back at the treehouse.

THE END

TOM, MINNA AND FINCH

BOOK 2

PATRICK WALLIAMS

TOM, MINNA AND FINCH

The day was sunny and windy, and Tom, Minna and Finch were running full tilt through the long grass. It hadn't started off as a race but it had turned into one, and Finch was in the lead.

"You're cheating, that's why!" Tom shouted.

All three were out of breath by now, then suddenly Finch tumbled headfirst into the long grass and lay there holding his leg and groaning.

Tom and Minna slowed to a standstill and dashed over to see what had happened. Finch lay there holding his leg, groaning and staring at the blood that was running down his leg.

"Poor Finch! You're bleeding," Minna said anxiously, kneeling down beside her brother.

"What on earth happened?" demanded Tom in amazement.

"It's cut!" Finch said, the blood running from between his fingers.

"It's cut really bad," said Minna anxiously.

"We need a dock leaf!" said Tom. He looked all round and quickly found a big shiny dock leaf.

"Wrap this around it!" he said, "and hold it tight!"

Minna wrapped the big shiny leaf round Finch's leg and held it as tightly as she could until it stopped bleeding.

"Look, this is what cut it! String!" said Tom suddenly, holding up a long strand of coloured string he had found.

"It's not string exactly," said Minna, "It's too thin... and it's a really weird colour, isn't it?"

"I'm going to find out where it comes from!" said Tom firmly and dashed off.

"And I'm going to find out where it *GOES* to!" said Finch limping off in the opposite direction still groaning a bit.

"I bet that string goes right the way around the world and joins up around the other side! In a bow!' said Minna.

Minna was rather proud of her little joke, and she was sorry that the others hadn't heard it. But they hadn't. They had already gone. And they didn't come back for ages. Minna sprawled out in the long, long grass and stared up into the cloudless sky. She thought about Finch and Tom. And about the forest where they lived and about the hollow tree they lived in.

The tree was nearly a thousand years old. It hadn't always been hollow of course. The front door and all the windows, and most of the furniture too, had been made for them by Beany. Beany was their granddad and lived on the other side of the forest. Apart from making things he was also a magician.

His spells didn't work every single time, it's true, but he was quite famous locally. Minna began to daydream. Then suddenly Tom got back. He looked a bit grumpy.

"That string, or whatever it was, didn't go anywhere, it snapped off when it got to the fence," he said, and flopped down in the long grass.

"I wonder where Finch is?" said Minna.

They called him for ages and then, suddenly, there he was. He was still limping a bit, and he was carrying the biggest kite you ever saw.

"Found this!" he said, and flung himself down in the long cool grass beside Tom and Minna.

The kite, which was enormous, was made of coloured materials, which were all the colours of the rainbow, plus a few they had never seen before. Tom and Minna stared at it in amazement, in fact they were too amazed to say anything for a moment or two, Then Minna began to examine it very carefully.

"Just look how beautifully it's made!" she said.

"Our kite's the best ever!" said Tom.

"MY kite, truth to tell," said Finch, "since it was me who found it. And 'coz it was me who lost all that blood too!"

"It's ALL of our kite!" said Minna firmly, putting her arms around it, "and I'm going to look after it!"

They spent ages trying to fly it, but there wasn't a puff of wind... not one single puff.

So they trudged home. They took it in turn to carry it because it was quite big and heavy. Later Minna hid it under her bed where she thought it would be safe.

Well, day followed day and there was still no puff of a breeze. Not one puff. All three of them spent long hours staring up at the sky, hoping for some sign of wind moving about among the boughs of the trees, or chasing the clouds above, but there was none. The weeks went by and then, one night, there was a terrible storm. The wind roared down the chimney of their tree house, and battered at the doors, and threw itself at the windows and rattled them in their frames. Tom and Minna and Finch could feel the tree moving about, and listened to the branches and boughs moaning and groaning as the wind whistled and shrieked.

Finch was the first to wake up next morning. He slipped quickly out of bed and grabbed the kite before the others could stop him.

"Where are you going?" shouted Minna.

"Nowhere!" said Finch.

"What's that you've got?" yelled Tom.

"Nothing!" said Finch.

He dashed out through the door and was away before the others could stop him. He didn't even have his shoes on. He could hear the others shouting and calling his name and he laughed. The ground was littered, all around, with leaves and twigs and even a few branches, and the wind was still blowing strongly.

It is no easy matter to put a kite together in a gale. It pulled this way and that, and reared up like a horse and it was much bigger than Finch. As soon as the wind caught it, it began to race away over the grass, pulling Finch after it at top speed.

Of course he should have let go the moment he realized the kite was stronger than he was, but he didn't. He hung on, and followed after it, digging in his heels whenever he could, but only for a moment, for the wind would give a sudden mighty heave, and Finch would be dragged along as before, running faster and faster and taking gigantic leaps.

The leaps became more and more gigantic as the kite rose up, and Finch cleared first a stream, and next a six-foot hedge, and after that a whole herd of brown and white cows who panicked and went charging round and round in circles. Finch, at this moment became really frightened. The kite rose yet higher into the air and Finch hung on for dear life and closed his eyes as tight as he could.

He was carried, miles up in the air, to the part of the forest that he didn't really know, the part known as the Dark Heart of the forest where people hardly ever went because it was dark and spooky. The people in the village said it was haunted.

Finch opened his eyes, just for a moment, and all he could see was trees, spread out for miles and miles and miles all round, like the ocean. But he was losing height. He was heading for the tallest tree in the forest, a mighty oak, and he crashed straight into it. He spun round and round like a spinning top and swung to and fro like a pendulum. After a bit he opened his eyes. The kite was all tangled and ripped to shreds. Finch hung on tight to the tree with both hands.

He became aware, after a while, of a muttering above him, and he thought he caught the words 'some mad lunatic...' He wondered who the voice could possibly belong to so high above the ground, but he was, for a long time, too terrified to move an inch. At last Finch plucked up his courage and stared up into the tree.

A golden eagle sat on the bough above him staring angrily at Finch with his huge buttercup-yellow eyes.

"What brings you to my tree?" demanded the eagle. And the huge yellow eyes stared and stared at Finch, and the pupils became now huge and now little and now huge again as the bird spoke. Finch found this a bit of a worry at first.

"Beg pardon, Sir," said Finch apologetically. "You see the wind just carried me here with my kite... it just wouldn't stop!"

"I do hope I didn't do any damage to your nest," said Finch sincerely, and he nearly added "your majesty," for the bird was so very regal.

"Well, fortunately not," said the golden bird, "for there are three new eggs in it that were laid only this week!"

The bird hunched his massive shoulders and flicked his great forked tail, he blinked his buttercup-yellow eyes and he stared up at the sky, north and south and east and west, as the wind rustled his beautiful feathers. After a while he spoke again: "You are not very big and you are not very tall," he said, "and you rush about in the sky without any wings, but I can tell when I look into your eyes that I can trust you." He stared hard at Finch with his yellow eyes. "So perhaps it was providence that blew you to my tree, for I am going to trust you with the most precious things in the whole forest! These three beautiful eggs! For that great tempest carried away my wife above the treetops and she has not returned! Who knows what may have happened".

The wind rose up again at that moment as if it would blow him from the branch.

"I must go in search of her," he went on, "and you shall be entrusted with the care of the eggs! Come and see!"

The nest was very strongly made of sticks all interlaced together, and it was lined with moss and sheep's wool. The three eggs, within, were a lovely creamy colour with flecks of gold and yellow and black.

Finch felt very proud to be entrusted with the care of such beautiful eggs.

"You must sit perfectly still in the centre of the nest," went on the imperious bird firmly, "and spread your wings all around to cover them closely. But of course! You *HAVE* no wings... what am I saying?"

"You will have to spread your clothing all about them, and that will have to do. But do make quite sure that a *DRAUGHT* does not get in round the edges!" The Eagle gave Finch one more searching a searching look with those eyes and then with one mighty downbeat of his wings he rose straight up into the air, and away to the west.

Now, whether the Eagle had hypnotized Finch with his great yellow eyes, or whether he was exhausted after his terrifying flight above the treetops or whether the rocking of the nest had lulled his senses like a cradle, I do not know but he slept for hours and hours without moving a muscle, with those three precious eggs, as warm as toast, beneath him.

The next thing that happened was that Finch was wide awake. There were men's voices speaking urgently together beneath the tree. For a moment he could not remember where on earth he was... but then he remembered! The gale! The kite! The dreadful flight over field and wood and river and hilltop! The eggs!!!!!

The voices came again and, very cautiously; Finch leaned over the edge of the nest and stared down. A hundred feet below there were two men staring up at the nest with binoculars... one had a green anorak the other a red one.

"That the one?" asked the one in the green anorak.

"That's our baby!" said the one in the red anorak.

"It's a fair height!" said green.

"A hundred and forty feet!" said red.

"We'll have a bet!" said green, "I'll bet you it's three eggs!"

"Bet you four!" said red, "I'm goin' up... I got my tree-treaders on!"

Red sprang into the tree, and Finch was shocked to see how rapidly he climbed. He never had time to be scared.

He waited until the man was only about ten feet below him, and then yelled out in the loudest and spookiest voice you ever heard. This is what he yelled:

"FEE FI FO FUMM" he yelled,
"I'll spill the blood any man
Who climbs this ancient forest tree!
I'll toss him to infinite!"

The man in the red anorak froze. "Who's that'?" he hissed. And his face went as white as a sheet.

"And if you should approach the nest
I'll blow you east, I'll blow you west!
I'll blight your dreams, I'll spoil your rest
I'll bring you harm like I know best!"

Finch yelled all this in a weird shrieking sort of voice that was not his own. It terrified the man in the tree. It even scared Finch a bit.

"Who are you? *WHAT* are you?" whispered the man. He clung tightly to the tree trunk like a baby monkey clinging to its mother.

"EVERYTHING ALRIGHT?" bawled the man in the green anorak, trying to see what was going on.

"I'll break your bones! I'll spill your blood!
I'll follow you with fire and flood!" shrieked Finch,

"I'll follow you! I'll kill all hope!
I'll send you down the slippery slope!"

"What are you? *WHERE* are you?" whimpered the man in the tree,

"What do you want with me?"

"EVERYTHING ALRIGHT?? WHAT'S GOING ON??" Yelled the man on the ground.

"And now I'll count from one to three
And you shall leave this ancient tree
Or off you'll go to kingdom come
FEE!! FI!! FO!! FUMM!!"

"One!" shrieked Finch.

"I'll go! Oh I'll go! I'm going now!" sobbed the man in the red anorak.

"Two," chanted Finch.

"I'm going now! Just let me go! Just let me be!" said the man, "I've a wife and kids at

home! I won't be back, so help me! I swear
it! I swear it!"

*"I DON'T LIKE THIS! WOTS GOIN' ON! I'M
COMIN' UP!"*

"THREE!" screamed Finch.

The man scrambled down the tree, snapping
off the branches in his haste. He fell the last
ten feet or so, and knelt on the ground gasping
and trembling.

"What's the matter, man? What's happened
to you?" demanded green anorak. "You look
terrible, man! You seen a ghost or something?"

"It's nothing! Nothing!" gasped red anorak,
trembling all over.

"But what about the eggs?" demanded
green anorak.

"What eggs?" mumbled red anorak.

"What do you mean – what eggs?" gasped
green anorak.

"There weren't no eggs!" muttered red
anorak.

"But..." gulped green anorak.

"The nest were empty! Damn crows
must've got 'em!" shouted red anorak.

"Crows???" whispered green anorak.

Finch watched the two men scramble away through the brambles. Green anorak had his arm round red anorak's shoulders.

Finch had never had time to be scared. And now he got the giggles. He stared at the eggs. "You missed all that!" he said to the eggs. "You missed all that 'coz you were in your shells!"

He covered the eggs with his body to keep them warm. But he still couldn't stop giggling. The more he thought about the man in the tree, the more funny it seemed. The way he had clung there, like a baby, promising to be good! Finch was still laughing when the eagles returned.

"Well, I found her!" said the male eagle, "and, just imagine, she was two counties away. Blown off-course by the tempest. But, tell me: how are the eggs?"

Finch told the Eagles the whole story, about the egg-thieves and how he had made them flee.

The four buttercup-yellow eyes gazed at Finch, and their gaze was full of love and admiration.

"You did well!" they said at last, "you did well, and if ever you have need of us we will come to your call!" And they taught Finch the shrill cry of the Eagle, which is more like a shrill scream.

"You must never forget that call!" they added, "for one day you will have need of it!"

Finch practised it all the way home... but not too loud in case they should think it was for real.

MINNA'S DREAM

It was midsummer, and they had celebrated it, as they always did, by having a midnight feast beneath the stars. Not that there were many stars, that night, as the sky was overcast and heavy with rain; it was very hot, and there was thunder in the air. They had overeaten, as they always did on midsummers eve.

Minna had gone to bed at the same time as the others, but could not sleep. For a start, she felt a bit sick, and the night was hot and close and airless. She threw all her bedclothes off, but felt sticky and half-suffocated; she tossed and she turned and, eventually, went outdoors to get some air.

An ancient yew tree grew on the bank next to the lane, it was said to be seven hundred years old; and there was a badger's hole in the mossy bank beneath it that was even more ancient than the tree. Minna sat down on the mossy bank where it was cool; there was not a sound to be heard except for the occasional rustle and flutter from the crow's nests high above.

Minna lay down on the cool moss and closed her eyes. No sooner had she done so when she heard the snuffle, shuffle, snuffle, of one of the badgers close to her ear.

"I hope it doesn't mistake my ear for a fat juicy snail!" she thought to herself, but, because she was so very sleepy, all of a sudden, she didn't really care.

"Sleeping under our tree tonight?" asked the badger.

"Mmmm!" replied Minna, who was already asleep.

"There will be thunder!" warned the badger.

"Mmmm!" said Minna again... she was already drifting off into dreamland.

The badger, who was a mother with five babies down below, deep in the badger sett, snuffled around her for a moment or two, then wandered off in search of things to eat.

The moment Minna was asleep she heard voices. There was a young woman and a young man, and the young woman was crying. Whenever there was a lightning flash, Minna could see that she had long, long barley-coloured hair down to her waist; the young man was curly-haired and broad-shouldered, and he was wearing some sort of leather tunic. It had a thick belt around it with a big brass buckle on the front.

"Don't cry, my love," he was saying to her.

But she would not be comforted, and kept saying: "Oh! But I be so afeared! I be so afeared!"

And he replied, "There's nothing to be afeared of my love!"

"But you are to be sent far away!" she said.

"For a twelve-month only!" he replied, "and then we shall be together again for always and always, I promise!"

"Then I shall wear a garland of green willow 'till that day come!" said the girl,

"But I be so afeared of that other thing, too!" she said, "That thing that be in your sack! Oh! How could you have stole it? We shall be caught, I know, for they will surely catch us, and that will be the finish of us both!"

There was flash of lightning, then distant thunder and rain began to fall in large heavy drops. Minna saw the young man put a protective arm about the girl's shoulder, and then she heard her crying again. "And I be afeared of the thunder, and all; I be so afeared of everything this night."

The Crows in the nests above were scared by the coming storm, and were moving about restlessly in the branches high above Minna's sleeping form. And then a small twig was dislodged, and it fell, from high above and struck Minna on the cheek. She nearly awoke, and half opened her eyes, and the dream faded. But then she turned on her side, and gave a deep, deep sigh... and the dream came back again.

The young man was kneeling down, now, and showing the sobbing girl what was in the sack. It was brimful of gold and silver coins.

"And I never did steal it," he was saying; "It was like I said, there were these two villains at the crossroads. And I was takin' the mead to where the fair was. A whole tub of it. 'Give us that barrel!' they said to me. 'No', said I,

and they showed me the knife. Well, I had no knife, and you can't run with a barrel of mead that size. And they took it and went away. When they got merry, they called me over, and asked me to join them and have a drink of the mead and I pretended to drink with them, but I only had a cupful. And they told me how they'd met up with a merchant and his man, and how they'd killed the man, and how the merchant had fled away into the forest. And they told me what they'd took, and showed me what was in the sack, all silver and gold, and were boasting of it.

"Oh, they were well-drunken by then, and then they passed out cold. Lying on their backs, they was, and their mouths open, and their eyes, too, but only the whites was showin', and snorin' like pig-hogs they were. So I took the gold... in payment for the mead, you might say, and now 'tis ours by right, and I be a'buryin it right here in the ground where the badgers do have their nest. And in a twelve-month, when I am back after my service, and the hurly-burly is over and done with, then we'll come again for it. And that will be midsummer eve, the next one as ever there was. The badgers will keep guard of it for us, my love!"

The girl was not crying now, and was lying quietly against him. "And we will go westwards, like you was sayin'," she said, "And we'll get a place where we can live undisturbed. A bit of land, and a cottage with it with a good thatch to keep us snug and dry in winter!"

The rain was now beating heavily upon them, and in the vivid lightning flashes, Minna could see them both quite clearly... she could have stretched out her hand and touched them. The girl's eyes were closed. The young man had one arm about her and the other clutched the bag of gold to his chest.

"And now I'm puttin' it where it will be safe for us!" he said.

He knelt down and thrust the bag deep down into the badger hole. "There," he said, "it will be safe there till midsummer eve do come again!"

He hugged the young woman to him; and both were soaked now, and the girl's teeth were chattering with the cold.

"And now you must go to your mother's house," he said at last, "and wrap up well in a good dry blanket, else you'll be carried off by the fever!"

The rain got heavier and heavier and Minna suddenly awoke.

She was soaked to her skin, and her hair and clothes were all stuck to her. The lightning flashed continuously, and the thunder crashed and crashed again, almost overhead. Minna knelt down on the wet earth, and poked her skinny arm down into the badger hole. The rain was running into the badge hole in rivulets and runnels, and she rummaged about in the sticky clay till she found it. She drew it out and wiped it on her soaking-wet skirt, and, when the lightning came again, she saw it was a gold coin, warm gleaming bright by the badgers whose fur brushed it and polished every time they went in and out.

"What are you up to, poking about in our hole? And all wet, too?" asked the mother badger, sniffle-shuffling close to Minna's ear. Minna showed her the shiny gold coin, yellow in the lightning, she was shivering.

"There's plenty of them down below," said the badger.

"And we turn them up a'plenty every time we open up a new passage way. It's no good to us, we call it 'unlucky metal' because it never brings good luck."

Then Minna told her about the dream.

"That's what we call a true-dream," said the badger, "because, you see, it really, really happened, years and years, and hundreds of years ago, on this very spot."

When Minna went back indoors, her teeth were chattering with the cold, so she covered herself up with all the blankets she could find. Next morning, when she awoke, she still had the sticky gold coin clutched in her hand, and it brought back the memory of the dream!

After some hesitation, (for half of her wanted to keep it as a secret), she showed it to the others.

"It's King Henry VIII!" said Tom, in amazement, staring at the tiny round head with it's crown on, and at the ancient writing all round the edge.

"You can even see the date!" said Finch, "look! 1515! It's more than five hundred years old!"

The three of them dashed down to the ancient yew tree, and threw themselves down on the muddy clay. After an hour or two they had a stack of Henry VIII silver and gold coin, and after that they spent many more hours polishing them.

FRUMBOOZILUM

There had been a gale and the ground was all covered with leaves and twigs. Tom trudged along, staring up at the windswept branches of the trees above. He had been a bit worried in case the rook's nests had been blown down, but the nests were fine and the rooks were flying about happily.

But then he noticed something else high up in one of the tallest trees... a great big enormous something... a kite perhaps? At first he thought it was a kite, and then he thought it wasn't. He decided to climb the tree and investigate.

Well, it wasn't a kite and Tom couldn't decide what on earth it might be, so he tossed the queer looking object down to the ground and hurried down after it. Then he rolled it up roughly and took it home.

When he got home he unrolled it again in the middle of the floor and they all stared at it. It was reddish-green in colour and had greenish-red spots.

"It's a hat!" said Minna immediately, "a giant's hat!"

At first Tom and Finch scoffed at the idea.

"But there are no giants left," they said.

But then Beany came in, "Well, there's always Caractacus Crumpet," he said.

Tom and Minna and Finch laughed at the preposterous name, then they all stared at him to see if he was joking. He wasn't.

"Who is he? Where does he live? Why didn't you tell us about him before?" they asked. Beany explained as best he could.

"Well he's a bit *STRANGE*, you see, and, well, he's very *BIG* obviously, and well, he doesn't go *OUT* very much. He lives on t'other side of the valley in what they call 'The Big House', which is really more like a castle. I only ever saw him once... and that was years ago. Funny sort of chap he looked!"

Tom decided to return the hat to its owner the very next day, and he started out really early. To get to the other side of the valley was a longish walk, and there were many streams and small rivers to be crossed along the way. The hat was quite heavy and awkward to carry, and Tom got puffed out and had to stop, more than once, to rest his weary arms. Once, while he was resting, a raven flapped down out of the sky.

"Cark! Cark!" barked the Raven,

"What are you doing with the master's hat?"

Tom explained how he had found it in a treetop, and how he was returning it to its rightful owner that morning.

"Heaven be praised!" croaked the Raven. "The master has been inconsolable since it blew away! A most dreadful temper, has the master, and that day he had a real *TANTRUM!* He shrieked, he bawled, he cried, he howled, he bashed his head against the wall, he booted the front door in... and then he threw Mr Pipkin into the moat! That was a real tantrum l can tell you! Return the hat to The Big House, midget, oh, hurry it there with all speed! I will fly ahead and give the master the wonderful news!"

Tom did not like being called 'midget', but he gathered up the hat in his tired arms and trudged bravely on towards The Big House. Because it was so very big, The Big House looked quite near, but it was not, and it took Tom many weary hours to reach it.

As Beany had said, it was really more like a castle than a house. There were enormous watchtowers with turrets to either side of the front door, and a biggish moat around the sides. The moat was largely filled with old rubbish. empty bottles, tin cans and cabbage leaves.

Tom stood before the immense door, and stared about him. He could not help noticing the boot hole in it... because it was a very large hole. I do hope he's in a happier mood today, thought Tom to himself.

He pulled at the bell-pull and was startled by the clanging and clattering of a big rusty bell high up in one of the towers. After a while the door was opened an inch or two by a tiny, wee man who was not much bigger than Tom himself.

"Welcome young Sir!" said the little man. "My name's Pipkin! Mister Pipkin! You have probably heard of me! I used to be quite famous years ago!"

Tom wondered what to say.

"Here, let me take the master's hat from you! What a blessing! What a Godsend! We already heard the wondrous news from the messenger, and the master was overjoyed, yes, overjoyed! He cried with joy! He danced with joy, and did any number of cartwheels and backward sumersaults. He has already set out to get some Potatoes!"

"Potatoes?" asked Tom looking puzzled.

"Why yes! Spuds!" said Mr Pipkin, "Tatties! And treacle of course! For he's preparing a delicious feast in your honour! A banquet! So come back the same time tomorrow for the most scrumptious, the most sumptuous, the most delicious feast you've ever eaten in your whole life! He's going to make frumboozilum!!!"

Mr Pipkin whispered the word frumboozilum and, at the same time, screwed up his face in the most extraordinary way, closing one nostril with his index finger, winking his eyes and waggling his ears. All at the same time.

Tom was not too sure what frumboozilum was, but he nodded his head. Mr Pipkin winked again, and Tom winked back: it seemed to be the right thing to do.

"Until tomorrow then!" whispered Mr Pipkin, "same time! Same place! Don't be late! Bye bye!"

"And he didn't even offer me a glass of water!" muttered Tom to himself, as he plodded homewards across the broad valley, his arms and legs practically falling off with tiredness. "Just catch me walking all that way again tomorrow for a bit of rotten old frumboozilum..."

But when tomorrow came, off he marched again, back to The Big House, because he just had to see his first ever giant. Minna and Finch wanted to come too, but Tom would not hear of it.

"You haven't been invited!" he said.

So there he was again, back at The Big House, standing under the midday sun, in a clean white shirt and with his coat and trousers freshly darned and patched and his boots polished up with beeswax.

He pulled again at the bell-rope and set the bell tolling high up in the tower.

"Carkl Cark!" called the Raven. "The master's been up all night stirring and stirring the frumboozilum. l saw the light burning all night long, and there he was, stirring and stirring with never a wink of sleep."

"Welcome young Sir!" called Mr Pipkin, at that very moment, tugging open the door and looking very flustered and out of breath, "the master will see you in half a mo!" he panted, "the frumboozilum is all prepared! He made it all by himself, you know, from a special recipe that was given to him by his Granny!" Mr Pipkin winked and, without more ado, Tom was led into the house and along an immense stone-floored passageway.

The house was full of the strangest things. There were big dingy paintings of grand ladies and gentlemen on horseback; there was a gigantic portrait of King Leopold the Large seated on a rhinoceros and riding into battle. There were suits of armour, some with arms and legs missing; there was a stuffed bear with all its fur coming out and, when Tom tried to stroke it, its ear fell off too.

"Oh, don't touch that!" warned Mr Pipkin, "it's a bit wonky!"

Tom looked about him and decided that quite a lot of the things he could see were a bit wonky.

The curtains hung in festoons and were all cobwebby; the stuffing was bursting out of the chairs and the springs were all poking through. Down a spiral staircase they went, and past the cave-like kitchen. It was as hot as a furnace! And what a horrible smell there was. Tom gasped. At the far end, (only it was difficult to see properly with so much steam swirling about) there was a cooking stove with a huge iron pot on top of it. From the pot, as from a volcano, there arose dense clouds of smoke and steam.

Caractacus Crumpet was even huger than Tom had imagined, and was wearing a chef's hat, which made him appear taller still. He was all dressed up in a chef's coat, too, but there must have been quite a number of blowouts and spillages before Tom's arrival, for his clothing was smudged and smeared all over with coloured stains.

He held a big wooden spoon in one hand and a dirty dishcloth in the other. "Dear boy!" he bellowed, rushing forward, "Dear, dear, lad! To have found my hat! and to have saved it and to have brought it back! How absolutely discumbobulous of you! How utterly, utterly hippopodulous! And to have climbed that mighty tree! It was positively perpendiculous from all I've heard! What tyranosauricaciousness you displayed that day Tommy! What... what absolute mumbojumbular piecrustularity!"

Caractacus Crumpet picked Tom up and kissed him on both cheeks and squeezed all the breath out of him. Tom blushed crimson and gasped for air.

"There I was, that windy day, as happy as a bee and without a care in the whole wide world and then suddenly whoooooooooooooosh..." Caractacus Crumpet blew into Tom's face so very hard that he had to close his eyes.

"WHOOOOOOOOOOOOOOOOOOOOOOOOOOO OOOOSH!" He did it again! "And the very next moment my hat was whizzed into the sky, all up among the clouds and thunderbolts! I was distraught! I went bananas! I never dreamed

I'd see it again ever, ever, ever, even if I lived to be a hundred and seventy-three, like Pipkin here, oh how shall I ever be able to repay you for your strombolipolicaceousness?"

"Pipkin!" he roared, "seat him in the place of honour!"

The Banqueting Table was a mile long... or so it seemed to Tom that day... and the table cloth, though full of holes, was beautifully embroidered all over with flowers, and scorpions and butterflies and leaves and goblins. There was a beautiful silver teapot with a dancing unicorn engraved on it, and a silver bread knife in the shape of a dragon with a twisty tail. Tom chose a chair that had only one spring sticking through the seat and quickly sat down on it.

"Will Sir have a little bread with his frumboozilum?" asked Mr Pipkin in a posh voice.

Tom nodded.

"Brown bread or white, Sir?" inquired Mr Pipkin.

"As it comes please!" replied Tom cautiously, seeing that there was only the one loaf.

"Crust or crumb, Sir?" asked Mr Pipkin, staring intently at the bread.

"Er, I think the inside part, please!" replied Tom politely.

"Half or whole, Sir?" asked Mr Pipkin, cutting away at the loaf.

"Half will do nicely!" replied Tom.

"Top or bottom, Sir?" inquired Mr Pipkin screwing up his eyes with concentration.

"Um, bottom, I think!" said Tom.

"Thick or thin, sir?" asked Mr Pipkin in his posh voice.

"Oh, don't give him that old rubbish, Pipkin!" roared Caractacus Crumpet, charging into the room with a gigantic pot filled with frumboozilum.

"It's years and years old anyway, that bread, put it back on the shelf!"

"There Tommy!" he went on, banging a silver plate full of frumboozilum down. "Get that down you!" he roared encouragingly.

"Get outside of that, my lad!" he bellowed.

Caractacus Crumpet and Mr Pipkin sat themselves down on either side of him, their plates piled high with frumboozilum, and began to gobble it up at fantastic speed. Tom tried a tiny bit of it and at once spat it out again: it was absolutely disgusting! He was nearly sick!

Caractacus Crumpet stared at Tom, and his eyes grew as big as dinner-plates. "What's the matter?" asked Caractacus Crumpet.

"I...I don't like it," said Tom in a whisper.

"What does he mean Pipkin?" asked Caractacus Crumpet, his face as red as a beetroot. "I... I'm sure I don't know," said Mr Pipkin in a whisper, his face as white as a sheet.

"He doesn't like the frumboozilum," whispered Caractacus Crumpet, blankly,

"HE DOESN'T LIKE IT! HE DOESN'T LIKE IT! HE HATES IT! HE HATES IT!" he roared.

Then SPLAT! He brought his huge fist down on the teapot and squashed it flat. The sixteen fat pussycats who had been snoozing before the fire fled for their lives.

"A tantrum, a tantrum!" they yelled. "Run for it guys!" And they shot out of the door in a volley like sixteen cannon balls out of a gun. Caractacus Crumpet stood up. He was breathing heavily and his eyes bulged and spun round and round like Catherine wheels.

"And I stayed up all night stirring, stirring..." he roared. "And I stirred it round sixty-four thousand eight hundred and sixty-three times, just like it says in Granny's recipe. And, and, and... then Tommy just comes along and, and, and, he... he just comes along and, and, and he just comes marching along, and, and, and he comes waltzing in here, and, he suddenly plonks himself down and, and, then he just suddenly turns round and he, and he *DOESN'T LIKE IT*," ZONK!

Caractacus Crumpet kicked a chair so very hard that it whizzed up into the air like a rocket and smashed into the ceiling with a crash.

"Calm yourself Caractacus!" implored Pipkin, leaping up and down. "He doesn't mean it! He doesn't hate it really!"

"He does, he does!" shrieked Caractacus and started to cry. "He hates it! He hates it! Boo hoo hoo!"

"But that's his sense of humour, don't you see?" shouted Mr Pipkin. "He comes from the southern part of the forest where everyone has a great sense of humour and everyone says the opposite of what they mean! Just to make everyone else laugh!"

"Do they?" sobbed Caractacus Crumpet. "Boo hoo hoo hoo hoo! Do they? So you mean when he says he *HATES* it, ha ha ha ha ha ha! He really means he *LOVES* it?" Caractacus Crumpet began to dry his eyes.

"Aye! That's the way it goes!" giggled Mr Pipkin, "Isn't that so, young Tom?"

Tom nodded. Caractacus Crumpet began to grin and put his handkerchief away in his top pocket.

"Tell me, Tom," said he, with a wink. Do you absolutely hate frumboozilum?"

"I really do!" said Tom. "I think it's the most disgusting muck I've ever tasted in my whole life!"

Caractacus Crumpet began to giggle. "Did you hear that Pipkin?" he asked. "Tom says it's the most disgusting muck he's ever tasted in his whole life! Oh. He's got a rare sense of humour has Tommy!" He began to laugh happily.

"I think it's the most disgusting slimy gunge in the entire universe!" shouted Tom getting carried away.

"Oh ha ha ha ha ha!" shouted Caractacus Crumpet.

"Did you hear that one, Pipkin? The most disgusting, slimy gunge in the entire universe! Oh ho ho ho ho ho!"

"It's worse than puke!" yelled Tom, beginning to laugh too.

Caractacus Crumpet fell backwards off his chair with a shriek and started to roll to and fro all over the floor.

"Worse than puke! Oh ha ha ha ha ha! Oh he he he he he!" he shrieked.

"It reminds me of dinosaur doodoos!" yelled Tom now getting thoroughly worked up.

Caractacus Crumpet closed his eyes and rolled to and fro, pounding the floor with his fists and kicking his legs up and down like a baby.

"Oh ha ha ha ha, he he he he he, ho ho ho ho... Dinosaur doodoos!!"

Pipkin now fell off his chair and together they rolled all round the floor in hysterics. Very quickly Tom got up and dashed to the window with his plate and tipped the frumboozilum down into the moat where some great big enormous carp quickly gobbled it up.

"Oh my ribs! Oh my poor aching ribs!" said Caractacus Crumpet later. "Oh that was a rare laugh we had!" said he. "What a party! What a feast! And look, young Tom has eaten every crumb! You must come here often, Tommy, and bring young Minna and Finch with you, and poor old Beany, too, he looks as if he could do with a morsel or two of frumboozilum!"

Tom thanked Caractacus Crumpet and Pipkin for having him.

"But you haven't had any afters yet!" said Caractacus Crumpet looking worried, "You haven't had any Prognostropus!"

"Is it one of your Granny's special recipes?" Tom asked cautiously.

Caractacus Crumpet nodded. "But however did you guess?" he asked in amazement.

"The boy's psychic!" gasped Pipkin in astonishment.

"I would dearly love to have some, but I'm absolutely stuffed full, and I couldn't eat an atom more, much as I would love to!" said Tom in his politest voice.

"Goodbye then, and promise to come back soon!" called Caractacus Crumpet and Pipkin.

"Goodbye! And thank you for an absolutely tyranosauricacious day!" said Tom.

"It was hippopodulous of you to come, Tommy!" replied Caractacus Crumpet giving Tom one last pat on the head with his enormous hand, "And it was absolutely tiddlypomtitudinous of you to return the old chapeau!"

"That's hat in French!" whispered Pipkin. "Goodbye, Goodbye!" they called.

"Goodbye!" called the Raven from the watchtower.

"Goodbye!" called Tom to the sixteen fat pussycats... but they stared at him with their disdainful eyes and flicked their tails. They still blamed him for the dreadful rumpus earlier that day.

It was well after midnight when Tom got home, but Minna and Finch had waited up for him. "I've kept some pie for you in case you were hungry," said Minna. "I made it myself from a special recipe!"

But Tom ran to his room and slammed the door. He couldn't stop laughing.

"What's the matter, Tom?" asked Minna, "We want to hear how you got on!"

But Tom had dived into bed and covered himself up in his blankets.

"I'm asleep! I'm asleep!" he yelled, "I'll tell you in the morning!".

LOVELY GREEN
MOUNTAINS

It had been blowing hard all night, and Tom and Minna and Finch were tidying up the leaves and sticks and bits and pieces that were strewn about all over the ground. Beany had his paints with him and was painting a little picture of the clouds and the sky above, The day was sunny and blowy and bright and the small white clouds sped across the blue sky.

"All the clouds are going north today," Finch observed, "Why is that?"

"Well the wind's from the south, see?" replied Beany, "so the clouds go with it."

"Where are they going?" asked Minna.

"Over the hills and woods and fields till they get to the sea." Beany replied, "and then on over the sea 'till they come to Wales and its lovely green mountains, and then on and on and on again."

The words 'Wales and its lovely green mountains' fascinated Minna. She could almost see those lovely green mountains, floating in the air, green and transparent, hovering before her.

"I shall follow the clouds and go there," she said softly.

'"Go where?" Beany asked sharply.

"To Wales and its lovely green mountains!" Minna replied.

Beany gave her one of his looks.

"I hope you're good at swimming then," he said, after a while.

"There's a bit of sea in between here and there," he replied.

Minna didn't say anything, but, to herself, she said, "I shall find a way, I know I will!" Beany went on with his painting, but glanced at her every now and then.

"Hope she's not getting one of her queer notions!" he said to himself.

Minna went up to her room at the same time as usual that night, but she didn't go to bed. She put on her warmest things and filled a bag with apples, cheese, and a big loaf of bread. She wrote a note to Beany, Tom and Finch saying she had gone to the lovely green mountains of Wales and would be back soon, then she squeezed out through the tiny window, scrambled down the tangled ivy stalks, and was off and away through the darkening forest.

There was a bit of a moon that night, and the bag bumped along on her back and felt warm and comforting, because the bread, which she had baked herself earlier that day, was still hot. The forest, at night, was full of queer shadows and strange sounds and as she marched along she whistled and sang to make herself brave. But every now and again she would stop dead and listen... to make quite sure there were no stealthy footsteps creeping up behind her... then off she would go again, singing and whistling.

There were streams to be crossed and hedges to be scrambled through and, as dawn lit the eastern skies and the first birds began to sing, she felt suddenly very tired and footsore. There was a haystack in the corner of the field, and she burrowed into it. It was as prickly and spiky as can be, but had a most lovely sweet smell, just like fruit-cake, Minna thought, as she dropped off to sleep.

The morning was bright and fair and the wind still blew. Minna brushed the hay out of her hair and her clothes, and headed for a little low hill, munching the bread as she went.

When she got to the top she gave a gasp of sheer pleasure and delight. Before her lay the sea gleaming and glittering and twinkling in the early sun. She half walked and half ran the rest of the way, and arrived breathless on the long shingle beach, which stretched away, away as far as she could see.

There were hundreds and hundreds of sea gulls, poking about among the stones, and a solitary fisherman was seated on a tree stump staring out across the blue water.

"Your pipe's gone out!" Minna said, and the man jumped, and took the pipe out of his mouth and stared at it.

"You gave me quite a turn then!" he said, "and what might you be doing so early in the morning?" he added.

"I'm on my way to Wales and its lovely green mountains," Minna replied happily, pointing to the distant greenish haze just visible above the hazy blue of the sea.

"I hope you know a friendly fisherman to take you across", the man said, "because I don't see how else you could get there... unless you can fly, of course."

"I have my own boat", Minna said grandly, "at least *I WILL* have very soon."

"Lucky you," the man said, "but whatever you do, don't you be tempted to land on any of the islands you may see along the way; there's bad people on those islands, so they say!"

"What sort of bad people?" Minna wanted to know.

"Witches mainly" the fisherman replied, puffing at his empty pipe and staring into the distance.

"Are all witches bad?" Minna asked.

"Who can say?" the man replied, "they say the witch of the east is a kind, good sort of person... cures warts and squints... all that sort of thing. But I wouldn't want to meet the witch of the west... they say she turns people into black cats... well that's what they do say anyway."

"I shall take care not to go to her island then!" said Minna firmly and, saying goodbye, she began to walk rapidly along the shore, looking about her, as she went, for logs or tree trunks which she planned to tie together to make a raft.

But suddenly she began to run for she had seen something that was so perfect she could hardly believe her eyes! It was a lovely pine door. It must have been the front door of a house because it had a name painted on it: 'Four Winds', and a brass letterbox, and a beautiful brass door knocker in the shape of a dolphin!

How could anyone throw such a beautiful door away Minna wondered? On impulse she knelt down and kissed the dolphin on its little pointy nose. All she needed now was a sail, and it was not long before she found one that was exactly right... it was an old umbrella made of brightly coloured panels, red, yellow, blue and green – a bit battered, but none the worse for that.

Minna pushed the handle of the umbrella into the letterbox; then she opened it, laid it on its side and tied its bendy ribs to the sides of the door with twine. She trembled with excitement as she looked at her completed raft. She tried to drag it towards the sea's edge, but it was just too heavy and would not budge; but the tide was coming in. It was not long before a wave surged forward, and a rush of white foamy water snatched the raft away from her. It raced away on the white foam, leaving Minna standing there. But only for a moment... for it rushed back again on another broken wave and Minna took a flying leap. She landed on hands and knees and grabbed the tilted over umbrella mast for support. And then the umbrella filled with wind and tugged at the raft, and the raft twisted around and began to move away from the shore. When Minna turned her head to look back, she was already too far from land to change her mind. She felt very happy and decided to christen her raft 'Four Winds'.

'Four Winds' did not sail gracefully, it bumped along, it chugged along, it lolloped along from one wave to the next. Whenever Minna sat down she got wet; but when she stood upright the raft would tilt over dangerously, so she was forced to crouch and hold tight to the mast for support. Some cormorants swam up and looked at her curiously, then dived out of sight; and later a school of porpoises went by, leaping high out of the water and calling to each other in their shrill reedy voices. Once a small sailing boat whizzed past and some people waved and called out to her in a language she did not understand.

The boat had a red, white and blue flag, so Minna decided it was probably French. She smiled and waved, and shouted, "Fromage! Fromage!" which was the only French word she knew.

"Bonjour! Bonjour!" they cried, and laughed and waved. Soon they were out of sight.

Then she noticed the island. It was only a little distance away, and 'Four Winds' was sailing towards it quite quickly. Meg tried her best to steer her little raft to left or right of the island, but nothing she could do made the slightest difference. 'Four Winds' went where the wind went – and that was that.

It was a beautiful little island; the grass was sapphire green in the bright sunshine and there were big granite boulders strewn about with flowering shrubs between them. The raft drew closer. Suddenly Minna saw a beautiful lady standing there in a sunny glade. She had long golden hair with a gold band about it, and wore a long robe of vivid blue… she was smiling and raised her arms.

"Welcome to my island!" she cried.

Minna didn't say anything; she kicked her legs up and down in the cold water hoping to slow the raft's progress, but it drew closer and closer to the shore. The lady in vivid blue walked slowly down to meet her, extending her arms in welcome. Her eyes were blue, and she had golden sandals on her feet.

"Welcome to my island!" she said again, with her lovely radiant smile.

"Is this your island?" Minna asked her cautiously.

"It is, it is!" the lady replied, "now come ashore, my dear, for you will be weary after your voyage, and hungry and thirsty too!"

Minna jumped off the raft but stopped with the water above her knees and stood with 'Four Winds' pushing her towards the shore. She was hungry and thirsty and stood there gazing at the woman in blue, and pushing against the raft with the backs of her legs.

"Are you the witch of the east or the witch of the west?" she asked, after some moments. The woman in blue threw back her head and the wind blew her long golden hair.

She laughed and laughed. "And what makes you think I'm a witch at all, at all, at all?" she asked striding towards Minna in her golden sandals.

"Now come to me," she commanded, "and rest a while!"

Minna stood there in the cold water, and wondered what to do. And then she saw a black cat step slowly out from behind a rock. And then another and then another. And from behind the rocks, and from out of the shadows, other black cats followed. And now there were scores of black cats, all standing perfectly still, all staring at Minna.

"How many cats have you got?" asked Minna quietly.

"Many!" replied the woman walking slowly to the very edge of the sea where the tiniest wavelets moved among the pebbles. Minna looked at her golden sandals and wondered whether she would walk out into the sea and grab her!

Suddenly Minna remembered a magic song that Beany had taught her. The melody had to be sung just right, and she sang it now, very softly: "Blow wind blow, blow wind blow, And blow the way l want to go!" she sang.

The raft suddenly stopped pushing against her legs. Minna repeated the song, and a light breeze began to blow gently into her face. And now the breeze filled the umbrella sail, and slowly the raft began to turn about. Minna jumped back onto the raft and slowly, slowly, the raft moved back towards the open sea.

"Au revoir!" called the woman in blue, her golden sandals at the waters edge, "l know that we shall meet again!"

Soon the South wind returned, and the little raft was swept along as before. It sailed between two small rocky islets, where grey seals lay upon the rocks. They stared at Minna with their big mournful eyes.

"Where are you going?" they asked her.

"To Wales and its lovely green mountains!" Minna replied.

"Oh don't go there!" the seals implored her, "for mountains are not real! They are made of nothingness, like mist and clouds and dreams and air! Only the sea and rocks are real!" Minna thanked them for their advice, and waved to them till they were out of sight. She leant her back against the umbrella mast...

... she was very, very sleepy...

... so very sleepy...

HMS PARADISE

And Minna... who had been asleep...
... suddenly...
... rolled off into the sea.

But the sea was only a few inches deep! Minna scrambled out of the water and looked about her. She was on another island. She dragged 'Four Winds' as far out of the water as she could and tied it up to a tree stump, then she looked about her. There was a haze of blue smoke rising up from among the trees, and there was a very nice smell: a combination of cooked fish and wood smoke. Minna followed the scent until she came to a clearing in the trees. There was a fire in the centre of the clearing and a man was poking at it with a stick and singing.

"Oh, there's some that sails to Timbuctoo
And some that sails to France
And there's some that sails to the Western Sea
Where the Whales and Dolphins dance
Fill the sails, bold Tempests!

BLOW! BLOW! Winds BLOW!"

He jumped up when he saw Minna. "Welcome aboard!" he cried. "You must have come in answer to the advert?"

He was quite old and skinny and tanned. He had glasses without any glass in them, and was wearing shorts, a T-shirt advertising Torch Batteries and a baseball cap with the word Coca Cola printed on it in red. All his clothes were very much faded and torn and patched.

"The advert?" Minna asked, looking puzzled.

"Why yes, laddie, I wrote an advert for a lookout boy, you see? I put it in a bottle, and threw it as far out to sea as I possibly could! I take it you *ARE* a boy?" he asked, looking worried for a moment. Minna nodded.

"Only your hair's a bit *LONG*... and a bit *CURLY*... and you're very *SMALL*, I must say... not that I can tell really! I'm as blind as a bat after that confounded tempest blew the windows out of my confounded spectaculars!"

Minna wondered why he called his spectacles his 'spectaculars'.

"Why is it so important that I should be a boy?" she asked.

"Well girls are so uncoordinated, and so... stuffed full of nonsense and daydreams and... all that sort of thing. A lookout boy has to have his wits about him... don't you agree?"

Minna nodded cautiously, "yes, I suppose so," she said doubtfully.

"Aye aye Sir, is what you should have said!" said the old man gravely, "I'm Captain Fawcet," he added, "I was a real live sea-captain once, would you believe it, in the Queen's Navy, but service life was too much for me... it did my head in! So one dark night I rowed away... and just kept on rowing! And this is where I ended up, on this piece of paradise... in fact I named her 'HMS Paradise'... not that she's a real ship, of course. And what's your name laddie?" he went on.

"Billy!" Minna replied, blushing with embarrassment.

"That's a good honest name!" said Captain Fawcet admiringly, gazing at her through his 'spectaculars'.

"Now then, Billy my lad", said he, "follow me to the lookout, which is where you will be spending quite a bit of your time in the years to come!"

"Aye aye, Sir!" replied Minna.

The lookout post was a tall tree on a cliff-top with a few planks nailed together at the top. Captain Fawcet handed Minna a big brass telescope, and Minna climbed slowly up. The telescope was very heavy.

"What do you see?" yelled the Captain, down below.

"I can't see anything," Minna replied, "there's no glass in the end bit!"

"Oh, blow the end bit!" yelled the Captain, "Try harder my lad! Screw up your eyes!"

Minna did as she was told, but could still see nothing.

"What do you see?" yelled the captain.

"A duck!" Minna replied after a while.

"A duck? A duck??" yelled the captain, "A duck's no good to me Billy my lad! Try harder!"

Minna tried harder. "I can see a boat!" she lied after some moments, "with a red funnel," she added.

"That's better!" yelled the captain, "Now come down and have some lunch before we both starve to death!"

"Aye aye, Sir!" replied Minna.

Lunch was boiled limpets. "The humble limpet is the finest food to be found anywhere on God's earth," said the captain, smacking his lips, "why, do you know, there was a ship-wrecked mariner on Rockall who lived for a hundred years with nothing whatever to eat but limpets! And when they brought him back to civilization he died in three days flat. Convenience food finished him off, you see! Stone dead!"

"Is there anything to eat except limpets on HMS Paradise?" Minna asked cautiously.

The captain shook his head.

"Although I do have a secret store with a few little luxuries for Christmas and festivities", he added. "You know, spam, condensed milk, that kind of thing!"

Minna had limpets, boiled, baked, fried, or roasted every day, for breakfast, lunch, tea, and dinner. Every day she would climb the lookout tree and gaze about her. She never used the broken telescope, and had no need to, as she had sharp eyes and a vivid imagination. If there was nothing to see she made things up. And when she made up something really exciting, the captain would dash off to his secret store, and return with one of his little luxuries.

Once Minna said she could see a clipper with thirty-four sails, and the captain dashed off and returned with a big tin of spam. Another time she said she saw a whale chasing a submarine, and that day he returned with a tinned Christmas pudding and some World War II custard.

Some days Minna would sit there, in her lookout tree, gazing at Wales and it's lovely green mountains; but, more and more often, she would gaze at the English shore, and think of home... and her eyes would fill with tears. How would Tom and Finch and Beany be getting on without her, she wondered?

One day, Minna made up something really spectacular.

"Anything to report?" the captain had shouted up to her from below, as he did, every morning.

"There's the biggest ship I have ever seen!" Minna replied slowly.

"How many funnels?" demanded the captain immediately.

"Three!" replied Minna.

"*THREE???*" shouted the captain excitedly, "What colour???"

"Orange!" replied Minna.

"Orange???" shouted the captain, "why, then it must be 'The Princess Maude'! I thought she went down years and years ago in the Western Sea! What an extraordinary thing! 'The Princess Maud'!"

"You are right," lied Minna, "I can just make out the name on the bows!"

"How very, very extraordinary!" gasped the captain. "What a splendid sight she must be! That telescope can't be half as bad as you make out my boy! Do you realise, m'boy, that the very cream of society will be aboard! Gentlefolk from every land! Lords and Ladies! Princes and Princesses! Dukes and Duchesses! Kings and Queens probably! The stars of stage and screen the world over! Why, I wouldn't be surprised if..."

"Oh, goodness!" exclaimed Minna suddenly.

"What is it?" shouted the captain anxiously.

"Another ship! And she's heading straight for 'The Princess Maude'... a real whopper... four funnels and..."

"Four????" yelled the captain, "What colour????"

"Red and black!" replied Minna, "And she's charging 'The Princess Maude' at full speed!"

"That'll be the 'Star of the Orient', but what crass incompetence! One could understand it if there were a fog or something! Are both the lookouts asleep??? Or intoxicated???"

"There's going to be a collision!" shouted Minna, her eyes shut tight.

The captain began to run to and fro, wringing his hands. "Oh, those poor people!" he kept saying, "Oh, those poor people! If we could only *DO* something! If we only had a radio! Or even a rocket! Oh, what can we *DO???*"

Minna suddenly opened her eyes... she had been in a kind of trance, and was really upset to see the captain in such a sorry state. "It's alright!" she shouted at the top of her voice, "They've seen each other! Yes, they're turning... yes, they've turned! They've passed each other! They've past each other with just inches to spare! They're safe! Everything's alright!"

"Oh, heaven be praised!" said the captain weakly, "Oh, heaven be praised! Come down Billy my lad. This calls for a celebration!"

"Aye aye, Sir!" said Minna, scrambling quickly down.

The captain dashed off to his secret store. Some minutes later he returned with an armful of tins. There was bully beef, condensed milk, spam, sardines and treacle. He lit the fire and mixed all the ingredients together in a big pot. It was absolutely delicious. Minna had three helpings and still had room for more.

That night Minna dreamed of home. She saw Finch and Tom and poor old Beany searching high and low for her in bogs and brambles and thickets and hollow trees in the deepest and shadiest parts of the forest. She tried to call out to them, but no sound came. In the morning she woke early. There was a strong wind blowing from the north. Minna tugged on her clothes quickly; she had to get home. She wondered whether she should wake Captain Fawcet, but she knew he would want her to stay, and was afraid he might try and persuade her not to leave.

She felt sorry for him, and left him a little note to say goodbye; then she sprinted down to the cove where 'Four Winds' was still tied safely. She pushed and pulled and tugged the little raft to the sea's edge and waited. And then a mighty wave came, and then another. It snatched them from the shore with a rush of white water. The umbrella-sail filled with wind and swung around pulling the raft with it.

Minna held tightly to the slender mast and waved goodbye to 'HMS Paradise'. Wind and waves together pushed and shoved and buffeted them along through the bumpy water. The spray soaked Minna to the skin, and she shivered and crouched down low, Willing 'Four Winds' to hurry on it's way.

By the time the shingle beach came into view her teeth were chattering with cold. It was the shingle beach where she had found 'Four Winds' all those weeks ago. As soon as she was near enough, she leaped ashore with never a backward glance. Everything looked the same!

The same fisherman was sitting there on his log as if he had never moved!

"Snakes alive!" he said, when he saw Minna. "Don't tell me you sailed to your blessed mountains on that thing?"

Minna had got so used to telling fibs that she very nearly said "yes." But she stopped herself just in time, and shook her head.

"Did you go to any of them islands I warned you against?" the fisherman asked.

Minna nodded. "Don't want to talk about it, eh?" he asked.

"Here, wrap yourself in this sheep-skin till you warm up." he said.

Minna huddled there in the sheepskin and looked at all the fishing gear, and at the fish that lay all strewn about, on the pebbles.

"What are those little ones?" she asked when her teeth had stopped chattering at last.

"Anchovies!" he replied.

"And that big fat one?"

"Bass!" said the fisherman.

"And those silver ones?"

"Cod!" he replied.

"That's A B and C, " said Minna dreamily. "The next one will begin with D, and then, just before you go home tonight there will be an E, a real big one!"

A moment later, there was a tug on the line, and the fisherman landed a dab. And, after that, just before he went home that night, he caught the biggest eel he had ever seen! It was a conger eel from five fathoms down!

"That sure was some weird kid!" he said out loud.

By then, Minna was nearly half way home.

THE BIKE

One day Finch found a bicycle wheel in a ditch on the other side of the lane. He had seen clowns and acrobats riding one-wheel bikes at the circus, and he made great efforts to ride on it... but after a couple of nasty falls he wandered off in the hope that he might find some more bits of bike lying about. After a short while he found a second wheel still attached to the frame. The wheels were exactly the same size. The frame had *MOUNTAIN BIKE* emblazoned on it in gold.

"Now all you need is some pedals!" said Tom encouragingly.

"Don't need 'em!" Finch replied.

Tom thought he was joking, but he wasn't.

"It's a Mountain Bike," Finch explained, "I'm taking it to the mountain, that's where I'll be going from!"

The mountain Finch meant was Mount Brocklehurst, which he could see from his bedroom window. It looked quite near.

"Then a couple of brakes might come in handy," Beany said, "in case you needed to stop one fine day!"

Finch was very happy with his bike and took good care of it, and practised freewheeling on the grassy slope behind the house. But, after some days, he got bored with this and yearned for the open road and adventure. He gazed longingly to the west, and to the inviting outline of Mount Brocklehurst.

"If I could start *THERE*," thought Finch to himself, "from the highest peak of all, I could work up such a speed I could keep going for a hundred miles! It would be perfect!"

Well, he set out first thing next morning. Before the others were awake. He didn't tell anyone. The day was sunny and hot. Finch had not realised quite how long it would take, pushing the bike ahead of him, to get to the top. He stopped more than once to quench his thirst from the mountain springs, and was glad of the apples he had brought with him.

A number of people on the road spoke to him in passing, either to remark that it was a hot day, or to comment on the steepness of the climb, and Finch would politely agree. One small boy asked him why his bicycle-wheels were squeaking so loudly, but Finch pretended not to hear him, and marched on his way, gazing at the lofty peaks ahead.

When he came, at last, to the highest peak of all, Finch threw himself down in the long grass and slept for an hour or so, with his arms hugging the bicycle tightly to him in case thieves should take it from him while he slept. When he awoke he felt refreshed and ready for anything. A gentle breeze blew, there was not a cloud in the sky and there were skylarks everywhere.

There was an enormous boulder at the very summit of Mount Brocklehurst and Finch climbed on top of it. To the north he could see more mountains, to the east and west there were forests, and to the south there were towns and villages. In the far distance he thought he might just be able to see the sea.

Finch considered his options carefully, and decided that going south held the most promise of fun and adventure. He heaved a sigh of contentment. Finch gave his bicycle a little pat of encouragement, then he took a deep breath and launched himself downhill. He had not realized how fast the bike would go on the road, and Mount Brocklehurst was very much steeper than the familiar grassy slope at home.

'*DANGEROUS BENDS AHEAD!*' read a notice, painted red, beside the road. The air rushed passed him as he approached the first bend, and made his eyes water. Finch remembered to lean to the left when he turned left, and to lean to the right when he turned right, but he didn't remember to put his feet down when going too fast – or, rather, he *DID* remember, but his legs were all bunched up beneath him, and he was too scared to move them.

"Oh, oh, oh, oh, oh!" he yelled, as he rounded the first bend; he skidded a bit but he didn't come off.

The hill became steeper on the other side, and Finch's eyes were watering badly. There were rocks and boulders to either side, and big clumps of brambles and nettles. The next bend to the left reared up before him and Finch leaned to the left.

"Oh, oh, oh, oh, oh!" he yelled, and again he skidded but didn't come off.

The road became even steeper. The next bend reared up, and then another and

then another. The next thing he knew was he was racing along, half in the ditch, and loose stones and pebbles were flying about and skidding and sliding under his wheels.

"Oh, oh, oh, oh, oh!" he yelled as he wobbled from side to side and from side to side and from side to side and from side to side.

Round the next bend there was a horse and cart right in the middle of the road. Finch went between the two huge wooden wheels of the cart and then between the horses sturdy legs.

"Heaven preserve us!", bellowed the farmer, falling backwards out of the cart,

"A Thunder-bolt! A Whirlywind!"

The carthorse reared up on her hind legs with a cry of terror, flailing the air with her fore legs.

But Finch was already rounding the next bend, and the one after that.

"Oh, oh, oh, oh, oh!" he yelled, for there, in front of him was the biggest and longest timber lorry he had ever seen... it was pulling slowly across the road in front of him... the big red cab passed before him, with its huge wheels, and then there followed the tree-trunks it was carrying, and then more huge wheels... Finch whizzed underneath *JUST* as the first pair of wheels had passed and *JUST* before the second pair had reached him... and they missed him by a whisker.

But Finch had his eyes shut tight, and he kept them shut tight as he whizzed along. He could not quite believe he was still alive, and when he opened them again there as another bend and another and another and another and another and another and another and another and then there came a very big surprise There were coloured flags everywhere! There were cottages with red, white and blue flags in the their gardens! And there were red, white and blue flags across the road too! Finch charged through the middle of them! There were hundreds of people everywhere... and the road ahead was full of children and bicycles... Finch sped through the middle of them...

THE BIKE

"WATCH OUT!!!!!!" he yelled at the top of his voice.

The children screamed in terror as he hurtled through the middle of them. One child crashed into somebody's garden, two into the hedge, three into the ditch, and four into the village pond where the geese lived. The geese were very upset. They had lived there for many, many years and had never seen anything like it before.

But now the road seemed to have ended, and Finch was bumping and bouncing across a grassy field... the grass got longer and longer... and Finch's bike got slower and slower and slower and finally Finch fell off on the soft, warm grass. How peaceful it was! There he was... lying in the lovely long grass... and his bike was lying there, too, a little way away, with its wheels still going round and round all by themselves... Clickity-click... clickity-click... clickity-click... click-click.

Somewhere, far away, Finch could hear a band playing. It was a village fair. From where he lay Finch could see swings, stalls, a roundabout... And now he could hear lots of people approaching.

"There he is! In the long grass!" someone yelled.

Finch shut his eyes tight.

"Poor little mite!" he heard a lady exclaim.

"Is he hurt, do you think?" asked another.

"He's a queer colour, poor little soul!" said another one.

"Ever so red in the face, ain't he though?" enquired another.

"Not dead is he?" asked another anxiously.

"He's fainted!" exclaimed another one sternly.

"It's the heat, more than likely, that's what done it!" said another.

"The heat! That's what it is!" agreed several all at once.

"Came first though, didn't he?" demanded another one.

"Better than all them others put together – in spite of his size!" said another.

"He is *LITTLE* though, ain't he now?" demanded another one.

"Not *BIG* at all really," agreed another.

Finch thought that if he kept his eyes tight shut they might all go away.

But they didn't. A man with a notebook and pencil came hurrying up, puffing and panting.

"Stand back everybody! Let him have some air!" he said bossily.

"Now then young 'un!" he said to Finch, "You won that race fair and square, so don't hide there like a ninny! The prizes are being given out in a couple of minutes, and we mustn't keep her ladyship waiting! You know how cross she always gets when people dilly-dally about!"

Finch blushed scarlet but did not say a word.

"What's your name, little-un?" asked the man, dragging Finch behind him as they hurried towards the brass band and all the people.

"Finch," replied Finch, out of breath.

"Finch what?" asked the man with the notebook.

"Yes!" replied Finch.

"Finch Watt?" asked the man.

"Yes!" replied Finch shyly. Finch was half pulled and half pushed up onto the platform, where her ladyship was sitting, next to the Lord Mayor and surrounded by red white and blue flags. Her Ladyship looked very hot, and the Mayor, who sat next to her, looked even hotter and was mopping his face with one of the red, white and blue flags.

"And First Prize in the Annual Bicycle Race goes, this year to little, to little..."

"Finch Watt!" hissed the bossy man with the pencil.

"Finch Watt!" repeated Finch, loudly and clearly. He really liked his new name.

"To little Finch Watt!" bellowed her ladyship lustily, "and a very thrilling event it was, l must say; little Finch Watt never dilly-dallied about like some of you youngsters did, but saw his main chance and, while one or two of you were shilly-shallying about, sped onward to victory!"

"Here here!" cried the Mayor, "Three cheers for little Finch Watt!"

A great cheer went up and the Brass Band struck up a rousing march tune when Finch stepped forward to receive first prize; "Bravo! Bravo!", everyone cried, well nearly everyone.

It's true one or two of the kids there called out rude things like: "He cheated!" and "He didn't even have any pedals!" and things like that, but they were told to shut up.

And the first prize, when it was, at last, presented was, (guess what?) A fabulous racing bicycle painted in fantastic fluorescent colours! It had a bell on one side of the handlebars and a hooter on the other, and there was a plastic drinking bottle in the middle, with an aluminium straw, ready filled with iced Fizzypop.

"Oh thank you mum!" said Finch in his politest voice, blushing with embarrassment and pleasure.

"Cheater!" shouted a fat boy with glasses.

"We'll get you after!" yelled a skinny boy with freckles.

"Yes! Just you wait and see!" bawled a girl with big red knees.

But Finch didn't wait. He whizzed off like a puff of wind. Soon he was miles away. He sucked contentedly at the Fizzypop as he sped happily homewards that evening, it was uphill nearly all the way, but the Fizzypop kept him going. And when it was all gone, he stopped and filled the plastic bottle with water from a little stream. The water was not quite as delicious as Fizzypop, but at least it didn't get up your nose the way Fizzypop does.

The others were having their tea when Finch got home. They were amazed when Finch showed them the new bicycle.

"How did you get it?" asked Minna suspiciously.

"Where did it come from?" asked Tom.

"Ain't it shiny though?" said Beany in amazement, "Just look at all them colours! I've never seen half of them ever before!"

Finch told them the whole story, leaving out not the smallest detail, except for some of the more dangerous bits he thought might scare them. They marvelled at Finch's cleverness, and asked him to tell it again.

"You should have brought the old bike home, though!" said Tom,

"I could never have brought two bikes back with me," replied Finch firmly "And, anyway, I told you, I saw some kids throwing it in the village pond... they said I cheated... they said they were going to throw me in too... they said I didn't even have any pedals!"

THE JIMMIE

Tom was digging for mugwumps in the soft brown soil. Minna had just about everything she needed for making a really monster pie except for one thing: mugwumps. Tom could not find one single mugwump, but he found a whole lot of other things... some rabbit bones, a curiously shaped stone, a fossil and then, just as he was about to go home, he found something unusual, something that was quite large and greenish in colour. When he scraped it, it shone with a goldish metallic glitter. Tom snatched it up and dashed straight home with it clutched against his chest.

"Look!" he yelled, completely out of breath, "Gold! Well l think it's gold... it looks like it!"

Beany put on his spectacles and examined it with care. "More likely brass", he said, after some moments, turning it over and over, "lt's a lamp, do you see, an old oil lamp, like they used to have in sailing ships in days gone by;

but don't be disappointed, Tom, polish it up," he said, "it will look as good as gold any day, if you make a proper job of it. All you need is a bit of elbow grease."

Tom set to work immediately, rubbing away at the greenish rust with fine sand and water. After sometime, the words 'Made in Bristol' appeared on the bottom of the lamp... but even though he rubbed and polished and scraped away for days on end, the lamp remained dull and lustreless.

"Put some of Beany's Turtle Wax on it", suggested Minna, at last, "Then rub it up with one of those silk handkerchiefs he's got!"

Beany was not there to object, so Tom set to work with the wax and the silk handkerchief without delay. Almost immediately the lamp began to gleam and glitter, and then, all at once, there was a queer crackling sound like electric sparks and a funny gunpowdery sort of smell... and then there was a shout and a chuckle... and there he was... a rugged seafaring sort of a man, standing there, as large as life, in the middle of the room, and rubbing his eyes, and laughing.

"Christopher Columbus!" he exclaimed. His hair was all tousled, his arms were bare and tattooed all over with anchors and hearts and sea serpents. His trousers were all ripped and patched and his feet were bare. "Well here's a to-do!" he said, slapping his thigh, and laughing, "What a fandango!"

Tom and Minna and Finch stood, rigid with fright, their backs pressed against the wall, their eyes wide with amazement. Tom was the first to speak.

"Are you a genie?", he asked, very quietly and politely.

"Well l be and I bain't, l'm a jimmie, do you see? A proper English jimmie, trusty and true!", the man chuckled again, and picked up the lamp. "And this be a good old English ship's lantern. Yes, there you are now! Made in Bristol! Well you can't get more English than that! Me? I'm Bristol born and bred... not one of your poncy Arabian smarmy-dick genies with their 'l grant thee three wishes, oh wise Master!' and all that carry-on, 'cos your trusty English jimmie don't bow nor scrape to any man, not like they Arabian greaseballs with their jewels and their flashy robes and that!"

"Don't we get three wishes then?" asked Finch after a moment or two.

The jimmie laughed and slapped his thigh. "Why, it's me what gets the wishes matey!" said he, staring at Finch with his bright blue eyes, "And me first wish this day is for a good log fire and a cup of good strong tea with sugar and cream in it!"

"But that's two wishes!" exclaimed Finch indignantly.

"No, no, that's but one, 'cos they be linked together, see?" replied the jimmie quickly. Minna dashed to the kitchen to make the tea, and Tom knelt to light the wood fire. Soon the flames were crackling and spitting and dancing in the grate.

Finch just stood and stared at the jimmie.

"Were you inside that lamp all those years?" he asked.

"S'pose I must 'ave been!" replied the jimmie.

"Weren't you bored?" Finch asked.

"S'pose I must have been... can't remember!" he laughed. "Now that's what I

do call a real good log fire," he went on, "But where's me tea and cream though?"

He sat himself down in Beany's favourite chair and stretched his big feet towards the blaze.

"What's your second wish?" asked Minna shyly, when she had brought the mug of tea with a dollop of cream in it.

"Why! A big fat slice of homemade fruit cake, and a clay pipe with baccy in it!" replied the jimmy rubbing his hands together and smiling happily into the flames.

"But that's two wishes, again!" said Finch.

"No, no laddie," replied the jimmie, "'cos they're tied together see, like I said."

Tom brought Beany's clay pipe from the mantlepiece and filled it carefully with fragrant herb tobacco from the jar.

"Were you a sailor once, in days gone by?" Finch asked, staring, fascinated, at the tatoos on the jimmie's arms.

"Well, I was, yes, and more besides, me lad!" said he, " I started off as a trusty Jack Tar sure enough, but fell into bad company, you might say. I became a brandy bandit a contrabander, you know... a smuggler! We used to bring in brandy, the best there was, from foreign parts. We brought it in by the coffin load, in the middle of the night mainly, and..."

"Why coffin load?" Minna asked, screwing up her face.

"Well, the biggest contrabander in the county was a Reverend, you see, the Reverend Peter Pennyfeather, who lived up at the rectory; well, we couldn't very well take all our bottles and barrels up to his front door, could we now? So we packed the brandy bottles in coffins, 160 or so in each one. Then we would drive them up to the Rectory, as bold as brass, in a beautiful shiny hearse, drawn by a black horse with a plume of black feathers on his topknot. Then we'd put the coffin in the lockup round the back. And that puts me in mind of my third wish, little uns, which is for a tumbler of brandy, oh yes, and a pair of carpet slippers for me poor old tootsies."

"But that's two again!" protested Finch.

The jimmie wriggled his toes and smiled at the flames dancing in the grate.

"We've only got Irish Brandy, I'm afraid," Minna said, dashing to get the bottle, while

Tom raced to get Beany's beloved carpet slippers.

"And now l'll tell you the most funniest tale you ever did hear!" the jimmie exclaimed suddenly, "And what a fandango that was!" said he, slapping his thigh.

"lt was a windy old, sunny old day, and we'd brought this coffin load of the best brandy ashore, do you see; well there was this other coffin, a real one, on the quay already. Admiral Archibald Armitage had just died at sea. The mainsail had come down on top him in the Bay of Biscay. It killed him instantly, of course, and they was takin' him to the Abbey, in London town, for burial.

"Well, we had such a party, us and the other lot, that we got merry. So what happened was we got the coffins mixed about and all our brandy, 160 bottles of the best... was taken up to London town and buried in Westminster Abbey!

"The King and Queen was there, and the whole caboodle, and blow me if they didn't put a great big marble statue on the top of it! It's still there I wager! 160 bottles of the best Brandy!"

"And what happened to Admiral Armitage?" asked Finch, looking quite worried.

The jimmie gave a shout of laughter. "Columbus confound us! We took him up to the rectory, didn't we though, and put him in the lockup round the back. Thought it was brandy see? But then, when we opened up coffin, next day, there he was, with his ginger beard, and that funny looking hat that he always wore, still on his head, and all they shiny medals and the lot! Well, we legged it down the lane like sparks out of a tar-barrel! That was a right old to-do I tell you!"

The jimmie laughed and laughed. "Oh, we had some funny old times!" he said, and he told them some more yarns, and tales of adventure on the high seas in days gone by. And Tom and Minna and Finch told the jimmie of their adventures in the forest, some of which they made up, to make their lives seem more exciting. But suddenly the clock on the mantlepiece began to whirr and buzz; it was twelve o'clock!

"Crikes! Me time's up!" exclaimed the jimmie gulping down the Irish brandy in one go.

"Must leave you my loves!" he said, wiping his mouth on the back of his hand.

"Will you come back again, if we rub the lamp?" Finch asked hopefully, but the jimmie shook his head, "Not allowed to. Tell you what I'll do though," he replied, "'cos you've gived me such a lovely merry evening, I'll tell you this magic word, see, a real magical one, and then if ever you really, *REALLY* need a friend, just you say it and I'll come to you. S'pose you was being chased through the forest, one dark night, by a horde of dingbats... you can feel their horrible, hot, stinking breath on the backs of you! Well, all you need to do is say this magical word, and I'll be with you in a twinkle!"

"What's the magical word?" Tom and Minna and Finch asked, all at the same time. The jimmie began to look a bit sleepy.

"It's mlunrumdlumrumbs," he said.

Tom and Minna and Finch all tried to say it but couldn't.

"No, no, no," said the jimmie, "You MUST get it right. mlungbmdlumrumbs... mlunrumdlumrumbs... quick, get some fresh ink and a good sharp pen and write it down in

THE HOLLOW TREE CHILDREN

your bestest writing." They dashed off to do as they were told. When they got back he was nearly... asleep and nearly... invisible. He was beginning to fade away at the edges.

"Mlunrumdlumrumbs," he whispered, "Mlunrumdlumrumbs."

"I think he's going!" said Tom.

"He's nearly gone!" said Minna.

"He's gone!" said Finch.

Then Beany came in.

He sniffed the air.

"Whos'e bin smokin' me best baccy?" he asked indignantly, sniffing the air. "And whose wolfed me best Irish Brandy?" he added angrily.

But, most of all, he was upset by the loss of his carpet slippers. "Them was nearly brand-new the Christmas before last!" he said. "I loved those slippers!"

DIRK AND BRAD

Tom and Minna and Finch were awakened early one morning by the sound of shouting and laughing on the other side of the lane; and then there followed a lot of hammering and banging. They snaked their way through the long grass to see what was going on. There were two men on the other side of the lane and they were putting up a notice.

Later, when the men had gone, they crawled through the hedge and had a good look at the new notice board. This is what it said:

NOTICE!
This is a Development Area!
It has been decided to level the land
in this area and get rid of all the trees!
Work will commence on Thursday at 9 am.

"If only Beany was here, he would know what to do!" said Minna.

"Well, he won't be back for weeks probably!" said Tom, looking really fed up.

"If only we had some of his Moonshine!", said Finch angrily, "Then we could vanish ourselves... and... and... go into battle! And beat them!" added Finch.

The three of them stared at each other... and thought hard.

"We are going to have to *MAKE* some Moonshine for ourselves," said Tom, "There's nothing else for it. We shall have to pit our cleverness and our magic against those horrible tree-people... whoever they may be..."

"There's a full moon tonight!" Minna reminded them. The three looked at each other silently and made up their minds.

That night, as soon as the moon was high in the sky, they got the copper mirror that they had found in the rubbish dump at the end of the lane, and they took it into the forest glade not far from the tree-house... it was made just as Beany had said it should be: "as flat as a pancake, but with a bit of a curve to it." They set it up on a tree trunk in the clearing, so that the moonbeams fell directly onto the mirror and then reflected back onto the rock-diamond. But no sooner had they done so, when a cloud passed in front of the moon and the whole forest was plunged into darkness.

"Oh! Why did *THAT* have to happen?" shouted Finch, beating his head with his fists in frustration. But an owl hooted to them in the tree above.

"Toohoo! Toohoo!" it called, "What's about? What brings you here at such an hour?"

Tom explained what they were doing with their strange-looking contraption.

"Don't be despondent!" the owl cried, "For the moon will be back in all it's glory!" and with that it flew swiftly away on silent wings. And it was true, for, within the hour, the cloud passed, and silver moonlight came flooding back once again.

Tom and Minna and Finch clustered round to watch the honey-coloured droplets gathering on the crystal, and drip, drip, drip into the saucer that they held below.

By dawn they had more than enough, and they poured the precious liquid carefully into

the little bottle, and screwed the cap on tightly so that it shouldn't frizzle away.

On Thursday morning a gigantic yellow tree-masher came roaring and wallowing through the forest, churning up the ground and mashing up all the trees and bushes that got in its way. It had two engines, one at the front and one at the back and a chimney on top for the smoke. The engines were turned off and two men jumped out.

"Nice quiet place Dirk!" shouted one, lighting up a cigarette.

"Not for long Brad!" laughed the other one, getting out the rope, the pegs and the red and white tape. "Not once we start shifting all these trees! Come on, let's get the line done! You got to start off with a good straight line! That's lesson one!"

They stretched the rope tight and, when it was good and straight, they knocked in the pegs.

"Straight as a die!" said Brad.

"Can't get no straighter than that!" said Dirk.

Then they climbed back into the cab of their Tree-Masher and got out the sandwich boxes and thermos flasks.

"Time for a cuppa and a sarnie!", said Dirk, "What sort you got today, Brad?"

"Prawns and mayo!", said Brad, "always have prawns and mayo on a Thursday!"

"Ham and mayo, that's what I got!" said Dirk.

"Chicken and mayo's best of all!" said Brad, munching. But suddenly he stopped munching. "Hang about!" he yelled.

"What?" said Dirk.

"That straight line we just done!" gasped Brad, "just look!"

"Crikes!!!" yelped Dirk, "it's all bendy!"

"There's no other word for it!" muttered Brad.

"*B-E-N-D-Y!!!* And how did *THAT* happen???"

"Must be some blinkin' kids movin' the pegs about?", suggested Dirk.

"I never saw no kids!" said Brad angrily.

They had never seen Tom, Minna and Finch, of course, since they had taken just the right amount of Moonshine to be invisible, or very nearly invisible, and they hadn't been wasting their time... they had been moving things about. Brad and Dirk stared at each other, then they got the rope out again, and the pegs, and the red and white tape and banged in another straight line. They squinted along the line to make quite sure it was really, really straight, and then they returned to the Tree-masher. But Tom, Minna and Finch had got in and had been doing things to the machinery.

Brad and Dirk brought out the sandwich tins again.

" Just one left!" said Brad.

"Same!" said Dirk, taking a bite.

"Crikes! That's queer!" said Brad, "My sarnie was prawn and mayo, right? But this one's ham and mayo!"

"And mine was ham and mayo, right? And now it's prawn!" said Dirk.

"And there's something else!" said Brad, "'coz my prawn and mayo was in a white bread sarnie and *THIS* one is... brown bread!!!

"There's something goin' on!" said Dirk, "'coz *MY* ham and mayo sarnie was in brown bread, and *THIS* one's in..."

"So *SOMEONE* ...or *SOMETHING*... has taken the prawn and mayo out of my *WHITE BREAD* sarnie and... and..."

"And put it in *MY* brown bread sarnie, and then..."

"And then, and then... put the ham and mayo ..."

"In your *WHITE BREAD* sarnie!" said Dirk.

"So *SOMEONE*..." said Brad.

"*Or SOMETHING*... said Dirk.

"There's something goin' on..." said Brad, "Something that's not quite right!"

The two men stared at each other.

"Crikes! Look at that!" said Dirk, looking out of the window. "That straight line we just done! It's all bendy."

"I don't believe this!" said Brad, as they put in another line of pegs.

"Hope this place ain't haunted!" said Dirk

"Better not be!" said Brad.

When they tried to get the Tree-masher started, the engine at the front tried to go one way and the engine at the back tried to go the other way. The tree-masher went round and round in circles till it over-heated and the MPV blew off.

While they were waiting for the engineers to arrive, Dirk and Brad got the cards out. "We'll play for money!" they agreed. "We'll use the empty tool-bag for the bank!"

Well, they waited all morning for the engineers to arrive, and Brad lost more and more money and Dirk won more and more.

In the end Dirk said "I've been robbing you all morning, Brad! It's not right! We'll split it fifty-fifty! The bag ways a ton!" he went on, "I'm going to tip it out so we can count it and split it down the middle!"

He tipped it out. Both men stared. "What's this then?" Brad was the first to speak.

"You joking me?" asked Dirk very quietly. The two men stared at each other, then at the heap of gold and silver coins.

"I don't get it!" said Brad. He picked up a gold coin and stared at it.

"It's Henry VIII!" he said, "it says so on the front! And there he is! And that's his ugly mug!"

"Mine's Henry VIII too!" said Dirk, "and it's got the date on it too! 1525!"

"Henry VIII – that's the geezer with eight wives ain't it?" asked Brad.

"That's the geezer!" said Dirk, "and then he chopped all their heads off, didn't he? One after another!" said Brad.

Just then there was a terrible din outside. Hammering and banging on the side of the Tree-masher, plus a horrible kind of screaming sound. Brad and Dirk dashed out to investigate.

But there was nothing. "Don't know what that was!" said Dirk.

Then Brad and Dirk stared in amazement at where the gold and silver coins had been. In their place was a little pile of brass buttons. Minna had found them just a few days before in the rubbish dump at the end of the lane. She had brought them home thinking that they might come in useful one day.

Brad and Dick nearly went mad... they marched up and down shouting at each other.

"You joking me Brad?"

"You joking me Dirk?" they kept yelling at each other. And they kept looking at the buttons, to see if they had changed back again into gold and silver coins. But they didn't.

"I hope this place *ISN'T* haunted!" said Brad, for the second or third time that day, "because, well, I think I told you, didn't I? About this mate of mine, Kevin? Well, like I said, he was doin' this demolition job on the haunted house down, the road, right? Big strong bloke, he was, 30 stone, near enough, solid muscle, and... well... this place was haunted, like I said! And it began to get to him, you know what I mean? What with the *VOICES* and everything! And his nerves was in pieces, I can tell you! Well, in a week or two he was down to 28 stone, if that! He was in a terrible state! You should have seen him! Well the doctors tried every thing! Nerve Pills! Every colour you can think of! But the voices got worse! They began asking those questions... you know? Unanswerable questions..."

"Like what's the capital of Bolivia?" asked Dirk.

"No, no, the *BIG* questions, the *BIG* ones, things that only the dead know!"

"Crikes!" said Dirk, " Well I'm tellin' you now, if this place *IS* haunted I'm doin' a runner! And I don't mind tellin' you now!"

Dirk tried to light a cigarette, but the flame blew out, every single time, even though there was no wind, and then the matchbox disappeared, and then he found the matchbox, but there were no matches in it, just a bumble-bee, and the bumble-bee was very, very angry and stung him.

"You was tellin' me about those Unanswerable Questions, Brad," Muttered Dirk, "which is the most scariest thing I ever heard. And I've been told Kevin's been gettin' even worse with his nerves???"

"Yes, things got worse last week, I know that 'coz I saw his wife only yesterday, and things had got worse. The voices just stopped. Just like that..." replied Brad.

"But that was good? They stopped? That was a blessing?" said Dirk.

Brad sighed. "Well it seemed OK... for a bit..." he said.

"But???"

"But then came the *SNIFF!*"

"The..."

"The house was empty, right? And Kevin was alone, right? Plastering! And then suddenly: '*SNIFF!*' The voices had stopped! The house was empty! Then, suddenly: '*SNIFF!!!*'"

"And there was no wind???" whispered Dirk.

"And there was no wind! '*WHOSE THERE???*' shouted Kevin! And then, again '*SNIFF!!!*'"

Tom, Minna and Finch were there, in the cab with Brad and Dirk, but of course they were quite invisible. Tom sniffed as loudly as he possibly could.

Dirk and Brad stared at each other.

Tom sniffed as loudly as he could, again.

"That weren't the wind!" whispered Brad and Dirk both together.

Tom sniffed even louder.

Dick and Brad made a run for it... well, they *TRIED* to make a run for it but their shoe laces had been tied together, and they fell over, and the harder they *TRIED* to run the more they fell over.

Then Tom and Minna and Finch all screamed at the tops of their voices. And it was the loudest scream you ever heard. And the reason they screamed was because they knew that if they *DIDN'T* scream they would get the giggles! And they kept on screaming until they were sick... at least Finch was... but even then they *STILL* didn't stop. At last, when they *DID* stop, their tummies ached.

Minna dried her eyes on the dishcloth. "I can't *WAIT* to tell Beany!" she said.

"Beany will be so proud of us!" said Tom.

"He will wish he had been there!" said Finch.

"He will probably be a tiny bit envious!" said Minna who was still dabbing her eyes.

CANNONBALL

Tom and Minna and Finch did not go very often to the village as people tended to stare at them and them and to ask awkward questions. Questions like, "are you the kids who live in a tree?" Or, "how come you lot don't go to school?" But sometimes they would go at nighttime and have a wander around, in the pale light of the street lamps, peering in at people's windows.

Once, in the moonlight, they had walked along the rooftops and looked down the chimneys, and listened to the voices down below. Once Finch dropped a pebble down to see what would happen.

"Oh Blimie!" they heard someone shout, "look what's happened! Where did all that blinkin' soot come from?"

One night as they were gazing into the window of the village sweet shop, Minna noticed a little card that someone had put there among the sweets and chocolate bars. This is what it said:

LOST DOG!
SPOT, A BLACK & WHITE TERRIER
HAS BEEN LOST IN THE FOREST
REWARD FOR SAFE RETURN!

Tom, Minna and Finch were very upset about this as they had known Spot all their lives and they decided to ask Beany what they should do next day when he came over.

"Oh yes!", said Beany, with a sigh, "I saw her just a day or two ago... she was in the very heart of the forest... where it's really wild and dark..."

"But why didn't you tell us?" demanded Tom angrily.

Beany sighed again, and began to polish his specs, as he often did when he was embarrassed or lost for words.

"Well, it's like this," he said, "I didn't want you to get involved, see!"

"But why ever not?" asked all three together, "We know the forest inside out, even the heart of it, we've been there a hundred times!"

Beany put his specs back on and gave them a serious look.

"Well, it's like this," he said with a sigh, "it seems Spot has been took by a man… by a very bad, dangerous man… called Cannonball, and…"

"Cannonball! Why Cannonball?" they demanded in amazement.

"Well," Beany began, "his head is ROUND, like a cannonball, see? And not one single hair to be seen! And, like I was sayin', he's very bad and he's very dangerous, and I don't want you lot goin' anywhere near. He lives in sort of tent that he's made for himself out of bits of canvas… but the thing is, the whole area, round about is just riddled with those blessed holes in the ground that local people call 'chimblies'… in fact they are mines that prehistoric men dug thousands and thousands of years ago quarrying for flints."

The moment they were alone together, Tom, Minna and Finch began to plan how best to rescue Spot, and they dreamed up all manner of schemes, some more fantastical than others. To begin with they walked boldly into the heart of the forest, stopping every now and again to listen. Eventually they became aware of a sort of tuneless whistle... and they made their way towards the sound, being careful to make no sound.

The heart of the forest was very dark and very still... and no bird sang there. The tuneless whistling continued, and Tom, Minna and Finch soon began to find bottles and tin cans strewn about on the forest floor. They could plainly see Cannonball's camp now; it was just a clearing in the forest with a sheet of canvas thrown over the branch of a tree to serve as a tent. And they could see the remains of a tyre, and lots of bones strewn about on the ground.

Cannonball was sitting on an upturned crate in the sun. His head was shaved and he was wearing a sort of ragged army tunic, his eyes were small and pale, and he stared straight ahead, whistling his tuneless whistle. Cannonball's hands were all covered with purple and black tattoos and he held a knife in his right hand. Every now and then he would sharpen the blade, polish it for a moment on his shirtfront, then toss it high into the air. The knife would spin and twist high in the air, flashing in the sun's rays as it fell... then

Cannonball would lazily extend his hand and, without even looking, and casually catch it as it fell. Then he would examine it closely and polish it a bit more then throw it up into the air again...

Tom, and Minna and Finch looked at each other in amazement. Then, suddenly, they saw Spot. She was tied by rope to one of the trees.

Before the others could stop him, Finch jumped up and shouted, "that's not your dog! She lives in the village and her name's Spot!"

"Shut up, you idiot! " hissed Tom. But it was too late.

Cannonball sprang to his feet. "Scram you vermin!" he bellowed. Then he rushed at them like a bull, charging through the brambles and undergrowth as if it had not been there. He hurled a rock at Tom; it missed his head by an inch and struck a small tree, which it snapped in half with a loud crack.

Two more rocks were hurled at them as they fled, ripping the branches off the trees before crashing into the ground. All three sped through the forest with the branches whipping and lashing at them as they ran... and they did not stop running until they reached home. They decided they wouldn't challenge Cannonball again. Not during daytime at any rate.

But, one dark night, not long after their first visit, Tom suddenly said, "I think we should go tonight!" The three looked at each other and then, without saying a word, jumped up and dashed out into the darkness.

Because they had lived in the forest all their lives, Tom, Minna and Finch could see in the dark just as owls and cats can and it didn't take them long to reach Cannonball's camp.

"How will we know if he's awake or not?" asked Minna.

"Ssh! I can hear him snoring!" said Tom. The nearer they got the louder the snoring became.

They could see Spot now. She was still tied to a tree by a length of rope. They could even see Cannonball's knife lying there glimmering in the pale starlight. Tom picked it up and sliced through the rope with one single slice.

Spot was so delighted she gave a great yelp of joy! The snoring stopped and Cannonball came storming out of the tent.

"I'll get you this time!" he bellowed.

Tom, Minna, Finch and Spot fled into the forest. Cannonball could run faster than they could, and soon caught up with them... but Tom had a plan.

"We'll go back the dangerous way!" he said. The 'dangerous way' was an old track that nobody used any more. Right in the middle of it there was an enormous hole. It was an ancient quarry shaft. It had once had a covering to prevent people from falling in, but now it was open to the sky. Tom, Minna and Finch knew exactly where it was and anyway they could see in the dark. They were running full tilt now, and took a flying-leap, all three of them, over the top of it. Cannonball was only just behind them. Suddenly they heard him give a mighty yell, and they ran even faster. When they reached home they were exhausted and all piled into the one bed, even Spot.

As usual, Finch was the first to wake in the morning. He had dreamed that Cannonball had fallen headfirst into hole. And now he just had to find out. Had he, or hadn't he, fallen in? Finch scrambled into his clothes without waking the others, and sprinted off through the trees. Soon he was back at the quarry hole. He looked down. He could see a black shape lying there far below. The black shape was all crumpled up and was perfectly still... was it Cannonball? Or was it a deer perhaps? Finch stared and stared and he listened intently.

Then suddenly somebody, or something, seized him by the leg! Finch twisted round! A huge tattooed hand had hold of his ankle! And the hand came out of a ragged old dirty old sleeve... and the sleeve came out of thicket of brambles and branches.

"Let me go, let me go, let me go!" screamed Finch, kicking and lashing about with his one free leg.

Suddenly Cannonball stood up. He stared at Finch with his tiny pale eyes. "Got you!" he said, "I thought you'd come!" he said.

Cannonball started to whistle. Finch swung there, upside-down, his captive foot held tight in Cannonball's tattooed hand. Then Cannonball stopped whistling. "I know an

'ole a million times more deeper than this 'ole!" he said. "It's an 'ole that don't 'ave no bottom to it! The Devil's Chimbley they call it, and that's where you'll be goin'... DOWN IT!"

Finch shivered. Beany had told Finch about The Devil's Chimney, but he had never seen it. Beany had said it was a hundred feet deep, but that people in the village believed that it had no bottom to it, but that it kept on going down forever.

Cannonball set off along a forest track, whistling and swinging Finch from side to side. "Why?" asked Finch, "Why?" It was all he could think to say. "Why?" his voice was weak and his heart was pounding with terror. Cannonball did not reply, but turned off the track and began wading, waist-deep through the brambles.

"Where is it?" asked Finch.

"You'll see soon enough!" Cannonball replied, He was panting and sweat ran down his face as he ploughed his way through the tangled undergrowth. He began to whistle then, suddenly, he stopped. "lt's there!" he said.

There was the big gaping hole in the ground, with rocks and boulders scattered all around it. Finch felt a dreadful chill of terror in his heart.

"Why have I got to go down it?" he asked, in a weak voice.

"You can make a last request, a last wish," said Cannonball, looking down the hole, "and then it's down the chimbley with you... to the bottom..."

"But you said there was no bottom", said Finch, and his voice was weak with fear.

"lt's got no bottom as such", Cannonball said, "you jus' keep on goin' down it, forever, see?"

Cannonball stared at Finch with his little pale eyes and began to whistle again. "But Beany said there's a bottom!" said Finch, "And I want to know! And that's my last wish! I just want to throw a stone down... and hear if it hits the bottom... or if it just keeps on going down for ever and ever and ever!"

And then Finch remembered the call of the eagle!

Cannonball kicked at the nearest boulder, which was as round and as smooth as his own head. Down it went into the black hole.

Finch gave the shrill call of the eagle!

"It's no good you hollerin'," Cannonball said, "seein' as there's no one in the dark forest to hear you!"

Finch called again. Though he had practiced the call many times, he had never, ever, till this moment of terror, used it at full power... but now he did... just as the eagles had taught him.

Cannonball gave him a look with his little pale eyes.

"I told you!" he said. "There ain't nobody to here to hear you!" He gave a savage laugh.

But the eagle-call carried for many and many a mile and the eagles heard it.

"Holler all you like! I tell you, there's no one in this dark place that'll hear!" yelled Cannonball. He screwed up his pale eyes and stared at Finch. And Finch stared back at Cannonball... and beyond Cannonball... and there, high, high, in the sky, he could see dark silhouettes speeding down. And they sped on down on their huge wings, coming in, lower and lower. And they sped on down, all five Eagles together!

Cannonball never once glanced up, never saw the dark shapes descending upon him, so swiftly, from out of the sun! Then, suddenly, he was struck a violent blow on the side of his head by the first bird, and he staggered forward with a shout of shock and anger.

He stared at Finch, not understanding what had happened. Then he was struck a second time. He put his hands to his head and then looked at them... and there was blood all over them.

"What the..." he began, and he looked up at the sky.

And at that very moment, a third Eagle struck his face with all eight talons extended, and the blood ran into his eyes and half blinded him, and a fourth and a fifth bird struck him, and he began to run, one arm covering his eyes. And he shouted with terror and rage as he fled, blundering and crashing blindly through the undergrowth.

Finch looked up at the sky. He could see the eagles speeding round and round on their huge wings. And then they were gone.

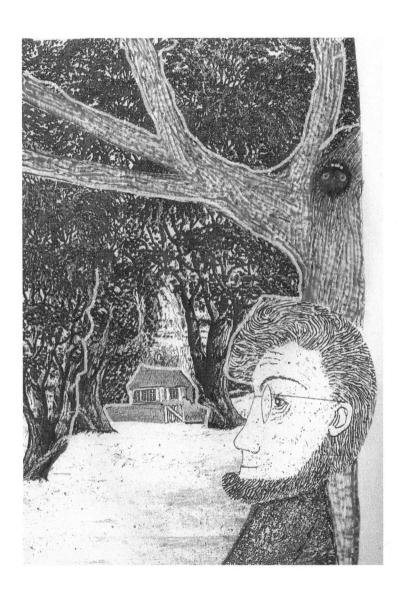

BEANY TELLS A STORY

It was evening, and Beany was just going out through the door when Minna spotted him.

"Where are you going?" she asked immediately.

"Nowhere special!" he replied guiltily.

"Can I come too?" Minna asked.

"And what's that you're carrying?" Tom asked him.

"Nothing!" Beany replied with a sigh.

"I'll carry it for you, if you want." Tom said.

"You're going to your hideaway, aren't you?" asked Finch.

"Oh lor!" said Beany dumping down the bag of tools he had been carrying.

"The fact is me roof's fallen in, and I've got to mend it before it rains again," he
said, "othenwise you lot could've come with me."

"But we'll help you Beany!" they all said simultaneously.

"Oh, come on then," said Beany, without enthusiasm, "but don't go blaming me if it's all damp and horrible when we get there."

"We like damp horrible places!" said Finch happily.

It was nearly dark by the time they got to his hideaway in the forest. Beany turned the key in the rusty old lock and opened the little homemade oak door.

"Oh lor!" he said. It was worse than he had imagined. Half the roof had fallen in, and everything was damp and dripping as it had been raining.

"Oh lor I...," he said again, "I need my head examining! I should never have brought you here, you should all be at home in your warm beds!"

"There's just one dry blanket." Minna said after she had hunted about for a while

"Then you three will have to share it," Beany said. "You'll just have to huddle together and keep warm... I'll just have to sit in me chair... I've got me pipe to keep me warm... if I can get the blessed thing to light."

He looked so miserable sitting there that Minna suggested he tell one of his stories.

"That will cheer us all up!" she said. "You start me off then," said Beany, still fidgeting with his pipe.

"Once upon a time..." Minna began briskly

"Once upon a time there was a man..." Tom went on.

"Once upon a time there was a very large man," Finch continued, "in fact he was so very large that..."

"All right, all right!" Beany said suddenly, "who's telling the story, you or me?"

He had got his pipe going at last, and was busily puffing out sweet-smelling Coltsfoot herb tobacco smoke. Everyone began to cheer up at last.

"He was really, really, *REALLY* large," Beany went on, "and he was rich, too, and he lived in a very large and very splendid house. He had a wife who was famous for her wit and beauty, and she had this lovely long, long golden hair. She was called Loropelia.

"Well every morning our friend would wake up at exactly nine o'clock, and call for his breakfast... today was no exception. The clock struck nine, and he opened his eyes at once. It was a lovely summer's morning. The sun shone and the birds sang.

"He rubbed his eyes. 'I'm awake, beloved!' he cried.

'And what will you have for breakfast today, my treasure?' replied the beautiful Loropelia.

'Eggs, my dearest!' he cried."

'And will you have them scrambled, fried, poached or buttered, dear heart?' she asked him.

'Some of each, my darling!' he replied, 'and I want them on my special red, white and blue plate!'

'Scrambled, fried, poached and buttered you shall have, my dear one!' she replied immediately.

'And served on my special red, white and blue plate, my sweet one!' he reminded her.

'And what will you have for afters, love of my life?' she asked him a moment later, when he had finished every scrap.

'Some boiled eggs would go down a treat, dear heart!' he replied cheerfully.

'And how many will you have, my angel?' Loropelia asked at once.

'One hundred and sixty-three, my dearest love!' said he.

'But won't you be sick, my sweet?' she asked him.

'I'll try not to be, my only treasure!' he replied bravely.

Well soon it was time to get up, and so he called for his manservant, Philboot, whose job it was, each morning, to put on his masters boots. This was no easy matter and took quite some time because, as I have explained, he was a very *LARGE* man.

'Are you quite sure you have put them on the right feet, Philboot?' Sir Humphrey asked anxiously, when both were on at last.

'Quite, quite sure, sir!' replied the faithful Philboot.

'Only they feel a bit funny!' Sir Humphrey complained.

'They *ARE* a bit funny, Sir!' Philboot replied gravely, 'They are your funny boots!'

'But I only wear my funny boots on Thursdays!' said Sir Humphrey peevishly.

'Today *IS* Thursday, Sir!' Philboot reminded him patiently.

'Then I shall go to the shops,' replied Sir Humphrey, and struggled out of his chair. 'Loropelia! he called, 'Today is Thursday, and I am off to do some shopping, my sweet one!'

'Take care, beloved!' she replied, 'and please don't fill yourself up with nasty old Fizzypop and sweeties!'

'I'll try not to, love of my life!' he replied.

'And please, please don't go climbing on any walls, my sweet one!'

'I'll try not to, my darling dear!' he replied.

Well, it was some ten minutes walk to the nearest shop, but Sir Humphrey ran all the way and got there in five minutes exactly.

He flung open the door and barged in, rather out of breath: 'Good morning, ten bottles of Fizzipop and twelve dozen Chocolate gob fillers, if you please!' he yelled, all in one breath.

'Why certainly, sir!' replied Mr Patel, 'and goodness me, what a very, very fine and lovely morning it is, Sir Humphrey, if I may comment, for a moment, upon it's climatological aspect.'

Sir Humphrey nodded, and crammed the bottles and chocolate bars into the bulging pockets of his coat.

'And did you notice the lovely new wall?' Mr Patel asked.

'What wall?' asked Sir Humphrey thickly.

'Why, goodness me, the very, very fine and splendid wall that the king, in his wisdom, has built about his new Wildlife Park!' replied Mr Patel. 'It will prevent idle and foolish people from gawping at all the wonderful beasts within, the zebras, and rhinos and thingmebobs, and all the other wondrous creatures. Why, goodness me, it is made of the very finest bricks to be found anywhere, and it is one hundred feet high exactly!'

'You don't say!' Sir Humphrey's eyes opened wide and he stared at Mr Patel.

'Where is this wall?' he asked almost in a whisper. Mr Patel pointed, and Sir Humphrey charged out of the shop.

The wall was even grander than he had imagined; it was not quite finished, and the workmen were having their tea break. An immensely tall ladder leaned against the wall and Sir Humphrey began to climb it. Because it was so very tall, the ladder sagged badly in the middle, and swayed about dangerously from side to side as Sir Humphrey climbed higher and higher

'I must be very, very careful,' Sir Humphrey reminded himself, 'and hold on very, very tightly.'

The view from the top was astounding. From where he sat, Sir Humphrey could plainly see the spires of three distant cathedrals... there was Salisbury Cathedral to the west, Winchester to the east, and Loonyville in between.

'Golly, I can see for over a hundred miles from here,' he exclaimed.

He took all the good things he had bought out of his pockets and stood the bottles of Fizzipop in a row on the top of the wall.

He began to sing, 'Ten Green Bottles standing on the wall! Ten Green bottles standing on the...' but even as he sang the well-known words, one of the green bottles accidentally fell. Down, down, down it went... and out of sight.

'I hope it doesn't hit anybody,' he said aloud, 'What a waste!' He kicked his legs about, and began to munch the Chocolate gob fillers.

'I shall keep the wrappers for recycling!' he said to himself.

He could plainly see the King's zebras, rhinoceroses and mammoths galloping about in the park below. They could see him too, and, in the Royal Palace, the Queen had also caught sight of him. She had been in the parlour, eating bread and honey, when she happened to glance up... and there he was... sitting on the wall with his back to her!

'King!' she yelled, with her mouth full, 'there's a weird-looking guy sitting on our wall!' The King was in the Counting House, counting out his money, when he heard her call. 'Eighty-seven thousand nine hundred and sixty-three; Eighty-seven thousand nine hundred and sixty-four; Eighty seven thousand nine hundred and... Oh botheration!!! You've done it again!!!' he exclaimed, 'What is it this time???' He came rushing in.

'Look!' the Queen said, she sucked the honey off her finger and pointed.

'It's that frightful fellow Sir Humphrey Dumpty from Dumpty Manor!' the King said slowly, 'I shall have to send a man on horseback to sort him out!'